"It's too late
for backing out,"

Joel told her harshly. "I've already spoken to Greaves and told him you're marrying me."

How possessive he sounded, Lissa thought wryly.

"And Lissa, one thing more," he continued. "Once we are married, I shall expect you to stay faithful to your vows. We live in a quiet village and—"

"And a front of respectability must be maintained at all times," Lissa finished bitterly. "If you disapprove of me so much Joel, why marry me? She could feel tears pricking her eyes and hated herself for her weakness. To bolster herself up, she demanded huskily, "And you, Joel, do you intend to keep your vows?"

"Do you want me to?" He was challenging her, Lissa knew, and feather-light shivers of alarm coursed through her body as he came nearer. . . .

PENNY JORDAN was constantly in trouble as a schoolgirl because of her inability to stop daydreaming—especially during French lessons. In her teens she was an avid romance reader, although it didn't occur to her to try writing one herself until she was older. "My first half-dozen attempts ended up ingloriously," she remembers, "but I persevered, and one manuscript was finished." She plucked up the courage to send it to a publisher but was convinced the manuscript would be rejected. It wasn't—and the rest is history! Penny is married and lives in Cheshire.

Books by Penny Jordan

HARLEQUIN PRESENTS

761—CAMPAIGN FOR LOVING
770—WHAT YOU MADE ME
785—THE ONLY ONE
794—THE FRIENDSHIP BARRIER
809—THE SIX-MONTH MARRIAGE
818—TAKEN OVER
826—TIME FUSE
833—YOU OWE ME
850—EXORCISM
868—PERMISSION TO LOVE
883—INJURED INNOCENT

HARLEQUIN SIGNATURE EDITION

LOVE'S CHOICES

PENNY JORDAN

injured innocent

Harlequin Books

TORONTO • NEW YORK • LONDON
AMSTERDAM • PARIS • SYDNEY • HAMBURG
STOCKHOLM • ATHENS • TOKYO • MILAN

Harlequin Presents first edition May 1986
ISBN 0-373-10883-4

Original hardcover edition published in 1985
by Mills & Boon Limited

Printed in U.S.A.

CHAPTER ONE

SHE was in a very dark, very smoky, very crowded room, crammed with unfamiliar faces, most of them contorted into frighteningly threatening grimaces. Panic surged through her in waves. She wanted to turn and run and yet for some reason her feet remained locked to the floor. Alien sounds and scents filled the air; she was overwhelmed by the despairing conviction that she could never, ever escape from the place of torment her inner consciousness told her her surroundings were, and then miraculously a door opened; light flooded the room and a man stood there his arms open wide to encourage her to run to him, his face in the shadows, but she knew without seeing his features who he was, and his name was torn from her lips on a glad cry as she ran for the haven of his arms.

'Daddy . . .' She cried his name again, her relief suddenly, horrifyingly turning to terror as he stepped into the light and she saw that he was not her father at all but someone else—a stranger—dark and forbidding, unknown to her and yet somehow recognised by her inner senses . . . recognised and feared. She screamed, and screamed again, and it was the sound of her own pain and fear that eventually jolted her out of the fantasy world of her nightmare and back to reality.

The nightmare. Lissa shuddered deeply, touching her damp skin with trembling fingers. It was years since she had been tormented by it—well three years at least, she amended mentally . . . since she had made the break from home and come to live in London. Sighing faintly she glanced at her watch. Six-thirty . . . There was no point in trying to get back to sleep now. She would have to get up in another hour anyway.

She padded through the bedroom of her small flat and into the kitchen busying herself making a mug of coffee. The fragrant scent of the beans soothed her sensitive nerve endings, the warmth of the drink stealing into her chilled fingers as they closed round the mug. It was still only January and the central heating hadn't come on yet. She shivered violently in her nightdress and pattered back to her room, sliding under the duvet; snuggling its comforting warmth all around her. Amanda would have laughed and said something silly, like the best way to keep warm in bed was to share it with a man. When Amanda said things like that everyone laughed. Her sister had a way of saying the most outrageously suggestive things with an innocence that robbed them of their sting. Even after three years of marriage and two children Amanda still looked like a little girl, with her mop of blonde curls and her large blue eyes. Or at least she had done. Deep shudders of mingled guilt and pain racked her as she sat huddled beneath the bedclothes. Dear God even now she could hardly believe it was true; that that midnight call three days ago had actually happened . . . That her sister, her brother-in-law and both sets of parents had been killed outright when a freak thunderstorm had struck the light aircraft her brother-in-law had been piloting.

She had not seen much of her sister since her

marriage—nor of her parents. There had been duty visits of course, but there had always been an air of uncomfortable restraint about them. She knew her parents had never forgotten, nor really forgiven her for what she had done. It was useless for her aching heart to protest that she was innocent. They would never have believed her. Tears formed in her eyes and fell unheeded rolling down her cheeks. Was she crying for her sister, or for herself Lissa asked herself cynically. She and Amanda had never been particularly close. There were four years between them, Amanda being the elder, and to Lissa as a child it had often seemed that whilst some Fairy Godmother must have looked down into her sister's cradle and given her the gift of a happy life; hers had been blighted by the machinations of some mischievous spirit who had ensured that she was destined always to be in trouble.

It had taken her years of exhaustive self analysis to understand that she was not to blame; that those things which she saw in herself as hopeless inadequacies because they did not mirror her sister's virtues, were not necessarily that. It was stupid to have the nightmare now, after so long had passed . . . Why *had* she had it? Why? Did she really need to ask herself that question, Lissa mocked herself. Of course not. She knew exactly why she had dreamed so horrifically of that party, of that long ago night, of Joel Hargreaves, her sister's brother-in-law, and now, with her, co-guardian of the two little girls who had been orphaned in the plane crash that had robbed Lissa herself of parents and sister . . . just as it had robbed Joel of brother and parents.

She had not been able to believe it when she received the 'phone call from Amanda's and John's solicitors. She had gone to see them immediately, taking time off work to do so, and had been stunned to hear of the tragic accident that had taken place while Amanda and John were visiting John's parents in Miami.

If Joel hadn't been looking after the children that weekend; they too would have been killed. Lissa shuddered deeply again. Even now she could barely take it in. She had had no idea until the solicitors told her that Amanda had appointed her joint guardian of the girls, along with John's brother, but it was not a responsibility she had any intention of shirking, no matter what the solicitors might think. Her mouth tightened slightly as she remembered the carefully worded comments of the solicitor, and his cool surprise that she should not want to extricate herself immediately from any responsibility towards the children. When she had taxed him about it he had coughed in vague embarrassment and then said half apologetically that Mr Hargreaves . . . Mr Joel Hargreaves, that was, had given him to understand that she would not wish to accept any responsibility for her nieces.

Lissa, who suspected she knew Joel Hargreaves and the way his mind worked far better than Mr Lawson, had seethed inwardly, knowing that what Joel had been intimating was not so much that she should not *wish* to take on the children, but that he considered her an unfit person to do so.

But she did wish to take on her share of the responsibility. She owed it to her sister and her parents—not to mention little Emma and Louise—

but it was not just that, she admitted to herself. There still burned inside a deep seated sense of injustice, an intense need to show Joel Hargreaves just how wrong all his assessments of her were. To prove that the great Joel Hargreaves was not as infallible as he and apparently everyone else liked to believe. And *that* was why she had had the nightmare . . . That was why she had dreamed so painfully of events which had happened more than six years ago. That was why she could not forget the humiliation she had suffered at his hands.

She sipped her coffee, refusing to allow her thoughts to slide backwards into the past. She had taught herself now to ignore the past . . . All right so she could not erase it . . . could not entirely put it behind her and close a door on it, but she could refuse to allow herself to dwell obsessively on it.

When she had come to London she had vowed to put the past behind her. She had fought valiantly against her own inner sense of inadequacy. She had found herself a good job, which she thoroughly enjoyed, working as a secretary cum P.A. to an up-and-coming young architect, Simon Greaves. She had bought her small one bedroomed flat, albeit with the aid of what sometimes seemed to be an extremely onerous mortgage. She owned a little car . . . took regular holidays. Had a pleasant circle of friends . . . never lacked dates. All in all, to the casual observer, her life was a very comfortable and modestly successful one. She had come out from behind the shadow of her elder sister, or so she had told herself . . . but did one ever wholly recover from the traumas of childhood. Wasn't it true that somewhere deep inside herself she still considered herself unworthy; inferior; judging herself as her parents had judged her, simply because she was not a carbon copy of Amanda.

Stop that! She abjured herself, pushing aside the duvet and padding towards the bathroom. She was wide-awake now and might as well get up. She had a very busy morning ahead of her, with a meeting with her parents' solicitors sandwiched in at lunchtime. She had already seen them twice and not been wholly surprised to discover that despite her parents, pleasant life-style they had left behind them few assets. The house had been mortgaged very recently to provide her parents with an annuity, which of course had ceased with their death, but it was not to discuss her parents' few assets that Lissa wanted to see their solicitors. It was to discuss her legal position with regard to her nieces. She didn't need sixth sense to guess that Joel Hargreaves would do everything in his power to have her guardianship of the girls set aside, but Amanda had stipulated that she wanted her as guardian to her daughters, and it was an act of faith and love that Lissa wasn't going to turn her back on.

Despite the fact that Amanda had always been their parents' favourite she and Lissa had always got on reasonably well. They had never been close, but they had always loved one another. In fact Lissa could only remember her sister being angry with her on one occasion. Stop it, she cautioned herself again. Stop thinking about that.

But it was easier said than done, which accounted for the fact that the past still haunted her in the shape of tormenting nightmares, even after all this time. At seventeen she had been so innocent . . . so naïve and trusting, but she had been judged as being wanton and wild, and the scars of that judgment still haunted her.

After she had showered, she rubbed herself dry briskly, grimacing ruefully at her mane of red-brown hair and her tall, slender body. Amanda had been small and cuddly, entrancingly feminine, whereas she as a teenager had been gawky and awkward to the point of being plain. Now when Simon called her elegant and classy, she was tempted to deny his compliments, to make him see that whatever elegance she now had was simply a disguise; armour behind which she could hide all her deficiencies. She herself saw very little to admire in her height, or in the classic bone structure of her face. Her hair which she wore long was probably her best feature, if one overlooked the fact that it was not blonde, just as her eyes were a cool hazel green and not blue. But then hadn't she realised long ago that she was not and never could be another Amanda. She was herself, warts and all. Sighing faintly she made up her face with practiced skill. The grooming course she had invested in when she first came to London at the suggestion of her first employer had taught her to re-assess herself as the person she was, not as a shadow of her sister, but she had stood in Amanda's shadow for too long to be able to wholly accept that she was capable of taking the limelight in her own right. The classic coolness of her demeanour was in direct contrast to her own inner insecurity, but few people guessed that. Not even Simon who was her boyfriend as well as her employer really knew what she hid away from public view.

Simon! Unwittingly Lissa bit her lower lip, marring its fullness with the sharp bite of her teeth. She had worked for him for eighteen months and for the last six they had been dating. She liked and admired Simon; physically he was a very attractive male, tall and blond with a ready smile and easy charm, but when it came to the crunch; when it came to the point of giving herself to him as a woman . . . of taking him as her lover, she held back. She knew that he found her sexual coldness towards him hurtful, but how could she explain to him that every time she came close to allowing a man to touch her . . . any man . . . she was instantly confronted by a mental image of Joel Hargreaves' darkly contemptuous features; and that the image was powerful enough to instantly quench whatever desire she might previously have felt. Joel as the mental guardian of her morals exerted a far more powerful veto on her ability to respond sexually to anyone than the most vigilant of parents. And it was all so ridiculous and unnecessary. The real Joel didn't give a damn what she did with her life; and anyway she was way, way past the age of consent at twenty-three. It was stupid and unnecessary that she was still a virgin. She heartily wished herself rid of the burden of her unwanted innocence, but every time she met a man she felt she could respond to, Joel came between them. She knew quite well why of course. But it was one thing to know, it was another to overcome the mental barriers created by the past.

'Stop thinking about that now,' she ordered herself. She would need all her powers of concentration today when she saw her parents' solicitors. She knew quite well that Joel would try to take the children away from her, to stop her from taking up her role as co-guardian. He had already flown out to Miami to arrange the funerals of Amanda and John and both sets of parents and he had taken the children back with him, all before Lissa had even been informed of the accident. The children were now living with him, and Lissa knew she would have to fight to preserve her own rights towards them. Quite why she was so determined to take up those rights, she found it difficult to say. It was true that she was fond of both her nieces; they were her sister's children of course, but she loved them in their own right. However, if Joel had not been her co-guardian . . . If John's brother had been a different man . . . a married man perhaps whom she liked and approved of, wouldn't she have been quite happy to hand the children into the care of he and his wife? Wasn't it partially because it was *Joel* who was her co-guardian; Joel her bitter enemy that she was summoning all her forces, all her rights under the law to oppose his high-handed decision to make himself solely responsible for the girls, by the simple expedient of arrogantly ignoring her co-guardianship?

What if it was? Legally she had every right to share his guardianship. Amanda must have wanted her to do so otherwise she would never have appointed her in the first place. But then Amanda would never have expected to die at twenty-seven. Neither would John, Lissa argued mentally with herself. No . . . she had every right to take legal advice and discover what steps she could take in the law to force Joel to recognise her rights.

What about the children? an inner voice argued. Was it fair on them to subject them to legal quarrels between their guardians so shortly after they had lost their parents? But if she didn't do so she would be cut completely out of their lives. Joel was ruthless enough to do that, she knew it. He was not married either, so there would be no feminine influence in their lives, if one discounted the string of glamorous girlfriends who seemed to slip in and out of his life, not to say his bed. No, the girls needed her, she was convinced of it . . . just as they needed Joel. Unlike him she didn't deny that he had his rights.

Simon knew all about her hopes and fears in connection with her nieces and had generously told her to take off all the time she needed to visit her solicitors. This morning she had managed to arrange an early appointment, which meant that she should not arrive at the office too much later than Simon himself, who didn't normally put in an appearance until ten.

The night before last Simon had taken her out for dinner and they had spent most of the evening talking about the children. Sighing faintly, Lissa finished her coffee and collected her outdoor things. Simon was intrigued by her she knew; he found her sexual coldness a challenge he was not used to facing; he couldn't see that her refusal to go to bed with him wasn't just a manoeuvre in a clever game, but a genuine abhorrence of the sexual act. She had tried to tell him . . . to explain to him why it was she found it so difficult to let him touch her even in the most general way, but as always, guided by some inner caution she had withheld the real truth. That was something she found it impossible to talk to anyone about, and a thin film of sweat broke out on her skin as her mind kaleidoscoped back and she was fifteen again. Clenching her hands together Lissa willed the memories away, but they refused to listen. How ungainly and insecure she had been at fifteen; how conscious of being the family's ugly duckling; of being unloved in the way that Amanda was loved. Her father had wanted a son and not a second daughter; she knew that, but even so, if she had been another blonde moppet like her elder sister she felt reasonably sure that he would have come to terms with his disappointment. As it was her dark red hair and tall uncoordinated frame were so much the antithesis of what her father thought was feminine that he had never been able to reconcile himself to his disappointment. Her mother, like Amanda, was a delicate, fluffy blonde, and Lissa had lost count of the number of times she had heard her mother explaining half apologetically to her friends that she had no idea where her second daughter got her plainness from. 'Not from my side of the family, I'm sure . . .' Lissa's mouth tightened, and she counselled herself sternly not to blame her parents. A more self-reliant and less intensely emotional child would soon have learned to come to terms with being second best. Her parents were not responsible for the flaws in her personality, any more than she was herself. Over the years she had taught herself to accept that and to make the best of what Nature had given her. There had been many men who if asked would have quite openly chosen her tall, red-headed elegance over her sister's blonde prettiness, but she had never allowed them to do so. Picking up her bag and keys, Lissa made for her front door.

Three quarters of an hour later she was seated in her solicitor's office, listening to his careful, judicial speech.

The question she had asked him was whether Joel Hargreaves could legally deny her access to her nieces.

'Not legally,' her solicitor told her, frowning slightly as he leaned his elbows on his desk and studied her. Her parents had been clients of his for many years, and he felt intensely sympathetic to this quiet, beautiful girl who he remembered as a rather plain and very frightened teenager. 'But of course, we can't overlook the fact that materially he can give them much more than you can. He owns a large house in the country, unless I'm mistaken?'

Lissa nodded. 'Yes, and he's rich enough to be able to afford a nanny for them . . . something I couldn't possibly manage . . . I know I can't have them to live with me on a permanent basis—at least not yet, but visiting rights . . . weekends . . .'

Her solicitor pursed his lips. 'Yes . . . yes . . . After all it was your sister's wish that you be appointed co-guardian of the girls. You're their godmother as well, aren't you?'

Lissa confirmed that this was so.

'It's just a pity that you aren't married, or at least engaged,' he added thoughtfully. 'Judges are often a trifle old-fashioned in their attitude towards minors. If they can see a ready-made family unit they look upon it very favourably.'

Lissa wanted to point out that Joel wasn't married either, but she did not. After all, unlike her, Joel could afford to buy all the help needed. Joel and John had both received all the benefits of

being rich man's sons. Both had gone to a famous public school; Joel had taken over running the family estate when his father retired, while John had run the components factory from which they derived their wealth. The estate was a large one, encompassing several farms, woods, a shoot in Scotland, and Winterly House itself, a Queen Anne gem of a building which Lissa had only visited twice, but had fallen instantly in love with. She had never been able to understand how John and Amanda could prefer to live in the extremely modern house John had had built for them, but then Amanda, unlike herself, had been a thoroughly modern young woman. Painfully, Lissa dragged her thoughts back to the present, in time to hear her solicitor saying that while there was no doubt about her legal rights to the children, he suspected that Joel Hargreaves intended to make it extremely hard for her to take them up.

He frowned slightly as he studied the papers in front of him, a faint tinge of embarrassed colour darkening his skin as he said hesitantly, 'And then of course there is the matter of . . . well, reputation . . . from the court's point of view . . .'

He got no further, because Lissa had stood up, pushing her chair back unsteadily, her eyes darkening to brilliant emerald as she interrupted bitterly. 'Are you trying to say that a court might not consider me a fit person to have charge of the girls? And how will they prove that I wonder?' Temper had her in its coils now, burning fever bright, pushing through the barriers of pride and reserve, words boiling up inside her and spilling volcanic-like from the place deep inside her where all her pain was buried. 'By checking through my

life? By questioning my friends? By delving into my private life, searching diligently for every little grub of dirt they can find?' Two angry spots of colour burned high on her cheeks as she added finally, 'Perhaps they might even want to subject me to a physical examination . . . just to find out how promiscuous I am . . . What a pity they can't apply the same rules and standards to Mr Hargreaves . . . but then of course, his lifestyle isn't important is it? After all he's rich and important, and I'm neither . . . Isn't that what you're trying to tell me.'

'My dear . . .' The solicitor looked and felt embarrassed. What she had said held a faint shadow of truth, although of course there could be no question of any examination of her . . . physical or otherwise . . . In the face of her bitter anger he felt unable to defend or even explain the workings of the law . . . nor could he entirely refute her allegations concerning the court's possible view of Joel Hargreaves. It was wrong and unfair he knew that.

'I won't give them up . . . I won't . . .'

Lissa turned round and almost ran from his office, still so angry that she never even noticed the speculative stares of his secretary who had caught her raised voice from inside her boss's office. No wonder she had lost her temper, with a mane of hair like that, she reflected half enviously. Her own hair was a soft mousy brown, and in her fantasy daydreams she had often imagined herself as a passionate redhead.

Lissa was still shaking when she reached her own office. Simon was there already, checking through the post. He smiled warmly at her,

checking when he saw her expression. 'Heavens, what's happened?' he questioned her, guiding her into a chair and perching on the edge of his desk. 'You look as if you're about to explode.'

'So would you if you'd just been told that you aren't a fit person to have charge of your nieces because you aren't rich enough to sway the opinion of the Judge.'

She was so overwrought that she was barely aware what she was saying, and unacknowledged, but at the bottom of her, agony was the memory of past hurts and humiliations and of one in particular so painful to call to mind even now that the thought of it seared her mind, making her shiver convulsively and grip her hands together.

Gradually Simon got the full story out of her, and then eventually said lightly, 'Well it seems to me that there's only one solution, and that's for you to get engaged to me.' He saw her face; and before she could utter her denial said coaxingly, 'Lissa, you know how much I want you . . . how I feel about you. Just give us a chance . . . If we were engaged I'm sure the court would be bound to view you in a more favourable light. Solid, respectable background for the kids and all that.'

He was offering her an engagement ring in exchange for the use of her body, Lissa thought sadly, and who was she to blame him for that? She had made it more than clear that she would never willingly give herself to him physically.

'No, Simon it wouldn't work out.'

Just for a second the mingled anger and frustration in his eyes frightened her. It showed her a Simon she had never seen before. She ought to have remembered that the powerful sexual drive that was in men to possess and dominate her sex could change even the mildest of them into a frightening stranger. She of all people ought to have known that.

'Because you damn well won't give it a chance to work out,' he swore at her. 'Christ Lissa, what is it with you? Anyone would think you were still a timid little virgin.' He saw her face and his expression changed, frightening her again as she saw the male satisfaction and victory in it, Exultation crept into his voice as he said softly. 'That's it isn't it? You are still a virgin? Oh darling...' He was smiling at her now, coming towards her. Any moment now he would be touching her. Lissa stood up shakily and edged away from him. 'No, don't run away...' He was practically crooning with delight and she felt sickness stab through her. She couldn't move... couldn't do anything to stop his arms coming round her, pulling her against his body. She went rigid at the intimacy of it, loathing him and loathing herself because she felt the way she did.

'Don't be frightened ... there's nothing to be frightened of ... I'll make it good for you, wait and see ... it will be so good ... so ...'

He wasn't really talking to her, Lissa thought with frigid distaste; he was thinking of his own pleasure; his own satisfaction. Held fast in his arms she felt as though she were two people; the frightened, terrified creature who couldn't break free of his hold; and then another, immeasurably older person who stood outside of her body and watched; censorious and cold, reminding her that she had no one but herself to blame for feeling the way she did. She shuddered with revulsion as she felt his hot mouth pressing against her throat. The outer office door opened and she was dimly aware of someone coming in, and then behind her a familiar and loathed voice drawled softly, 'Well, well . . . so this is how you spend your time these days is it Lissa . . . Nothing's changed then.'

Simon released her immediately, pushing his fingers through his hair in a way he had when he was caught at a disadvantage. Tall though he was, the newcomer towered over him. Few men could compete with Joel Hargreaves when it came to sheer masculinity, Lissa thought bitterly, turning round to face her tormentor.

'Joel?' She smiled thinly at him, grateful for the fact that she had somehow recovered her poise. 'As you say nothing's changed . . . You, I see still have the habit of bursting in on people unannounced. What were you hoping to find this time? Evidence to prove that I'm not a fit person to have charge of the girls?'

The wide male mouth slashed into an open curl of contempt. 'I don't need to go looking for that Lissa. It's all there, documented and collated and I don't even need to look for a witness do I? I saw the whole thing for myself.'

She wanted to cry out a denial, to hide away from the merciless scrutiny of his hard gold eyes, but she wasn't fifteen anymore and so she tilted her chin and said coldly, 'Your own personal life wouldn't bear too much close scrutiny Joel. People in glass houses shouldn't throw stones should they?'

He had a trick of looking at someone beneath those heavy lidded eyes that had always made her heart pound with a mixture of fear and apprehension. He did it now, making her feel as though he could see through her forehead and into the farther-most recesses of her brain.

'I want to talk to you,' he said calmly. 'I've got a busy morning but I could see you at lunch time.'

'And deny yourself the opportunity of lunching with your latest ladyfriend whoever she might be?' Lissa snapped. 'Don't bother. I've only one thing to say to you Joel and that is that I'm not giving up my rights to the girls, no matter what you say or do. Amanda appointed me as their guardian . . .'

'Silly, loyal Amanda,' Joel derided her sister. 'I'll bet when she did it, she never thought you might actually have to have charge of them. Your mother wouldn't have approved.'

It hurt because it was the truth, but Lissa refused to give in to the pain. She had enough experience of Joel's methods of waging warfare to know that he always aimed for his opponents' most vounerable spots, and he knew hers to a nicety.

'I'm not giving them up Joel,' she repeated coolly, 'And this is a private office. If you want to communicate with me, please do so through my solicitor.' As she finished speaking she walked past him and into her own office, firmly closing the door behind her. Two minutes later she heard the outer door slam and then Simon walked into her office.

'Phew,' he commented theatrically, raising his eyebrows. 'So that's the fabled Joel Hargreaves.'

Joel was constantly appearing in the gossip press. He had fingers in many financial pies and was known as much for being a highly successful entrepreneur as he was for his womanising. 'Quite a man,' Simon murmured.

'If you like the type,' Lissa managed a thin smile, 'personally I don't.'

'No, I could see that.'

Lissa hid a small smile at the smug satisfaction in Simon's tone. Physically, they couldn't be more dissimilar. Simon although tall was slim and boyish with his shock of sunbleached fair hair and his easy smile. Joel in contrast, was taller, broader, the epitome of everything that was intensely male. His skin was olive coloured, his eyes a glinting rich gold, his hair dark and thick. Once, rather fancifully before she had really known him Lissa had imagined that he might have posed for a statue of Achilles. She had always had an over-romantic imagination she thought wryly. Joel was no story-book hero. Far from it. Women fell for him like ninepins and he made full use of the power he seemed to have over her sex. Lissa had watched a procession of women come and go through his life, and if he had ever felt anything more than sexual desire for any of them, she had never noticed it.

'Dinner tonight?'

She dragged her mind back to the present and Simon. Over his anger now, he was a cajoling, eager boy again, but how long would it be before he reverted to type . . . before he tried to force her into an intimacy she didn't want to share. She sighed faintly. She liked her job and she liked Simon . . . but if he was going to be difficult . . . But how could she give up her job now, when she might need to prove that financially she was able to care for the girls, at least on a part-time basis. She knew there was no possibility of them coming to live with her full time at least not now. For one thing her flat had only one bedroom but in a few years' time . . . If, however, she let Joel bludgeon her into giving up her rights to them now; she would have no chance of re-establishing any relationship with them in the future. She knew that.

CHAPTER TWO

LISSA stared at the letter, tapping her nails absently on her kitchen counter as she studied its contents for the umpteenth time. It had arrived three days ago; a coolly worded, imperative demand from Joel that she present herself at Winterly so that they could discuss the girls' future.

Trust Joel to make sure he had the advantage of being on his home ground, Lissa thought wryly. The letter had surprised her; taken her rather aback. After the way they had parted in Simon's office she had expected only to hear from him via his solicitor, but instead had come this command, because that was what it was, to go down to Winterly so that they could talk. She was tempted to refuse, but if she did might that count against her in an eventual court hearing? Her solicitor seemed to think so. She pressed the heel of one hand to her aching temple. Perhaps she ought to take Simon up on his offer and hope that her status as an engaged woman might persuade the court to settle in her favour. But Simon wasn't really interested in the girls; all he wanted was to get her into his bed. She glanced at her watch. Ten o'clock. She had been up since seven, prowling round her small flat, knowing that she must go to Winterly but desperately searching for excuses not to do so.

Chiding herself for her weakness she went into her bedroom, hastily packing enough clothes to last the weekend, and then before she could change her mind, she pulled on a jacket, collected her car keys and carrying her overnight bag marched towards her front door.

There was a freezing wind blowing, driving needle sharp flurries of icy snow into her face, and Lissa huddled deeper into her jacket as she made for the lock-up garage block where she kept her car.

The traffic through the centre of London was bad enough to need all her concentration. Once on the M4 though she turned on her radio, and listened with grim foreboding to the weather forecast. A drop in temperature and snow, but not until late evening. Well she should be safely at Winterly by then.

Once off the M4 she drove carefully along the familiar country roads. She had spent all her childhood living in Dorset, the names of the villages she drove through composed a familiar litany. Her parents' old home lay only fifteen miles from Winterly. Amanda and John had met at the home of mutual friends, and the tiny village five miles east of Winterly she was now approaching was also the nearest village to her parents' old home. Nothing had changed, she thought with a hard pang of nostalgia as she negotiated the sharp bend in the centre of the town where the Tudor building now housing a bank jutted dangerously into the centre of the road. A sign outside a shop, fluttering in the cold wind caught her eye and she drew up outside it. A cup of coffee was just what she needed right now. Coward, an inner voice chided her as she climbed out of the Mini and locked it.

She didn't really want a drink, she simply wanted to put off facing Joel.

The small town was busy with Saturday shoppers, but she was lucky enough to find a small corner table still free. A smiling waitress came to take her order, the familiarity of her soft Dorset burr taking Lissa back in time.

She had just received her order when she heard someone call her name in an incredulous voice.

'Lissa, it is you isn't it?' the feminine voice exclaimed, a pretty plump brunette of about her own age hurrying over to her table, a wriggling toddler tucked securely under one arm.

'Helen ... Helen Martin,' Lissa exclaimed in turn, recognising an old school friend.'

'Helen Turner now,' the latter laughed. 'Do you mind if I join you?'

'No, please do ...'

Aware that Helen was studying her, Lissa strove to appear calm and friendly. At one time she and Helen had been 'best friends', but after ... but after she was fifteen they had drifted apart.

'I was sorry to hear about Amanda and John,' Helen said quietly at last. 'It must have been a dreadful shock for you. Joel has got the children hasn't he? Poor little things. They must miss their parents dreadfully.' She pulled a face. 'Somehow I can't see Joel in the role of doting uncle. Has he changed at all or is he still as masterful and macho as ever.'

'I don't see much of him these days,' Lissa said assuming a fake casualness. 'In fact I'm on my way to Winterly now. We're joint guardians of the girls.' She might as well let it be known that Joel wasn't solely responsible for her nieces' welfare.

'Yes, you're godmother to both of them aren't you.' Helen broke off as her son reached for his glass of orange juice, almost tipping it over.

'Are you married yourself?' she asked when she had rescued the glass. 'I remember I always used to think you would marry young and have a brood of children.'

'No, I'm still single,' Lissa told her calmly. It was true that when they were teenagers she had yearned for the security of a loving husband and children, but in those days she had been so ridiculously innocent, wanting without realising it to compensate herself for the lack of love in her own home.

'Umm . . . Well it can only be by choice,' Helen said frankly, wrinkling her nose as she studied Lissa's smoothly made-up face and immaculate hair. 'You look very lovely and elegant Lissa, I hardly recognised you at first. What have you been doing with yourself? I know your parents sent you away to school . . .' She grimaced faintly. 'And it was all my fault really wasn't it? If I hadn't persuaded you to go to that party with me. My parents gave me hell for that, I can tell you. What exactly happened?' she asked curiously.

'Oh nothing much.' Lissa was proud of her cool offhand tone. 'It was all very much a storm in a teacup.'

'Yes, that's what my parents thought,' Helen agreed. 'I remember them discussing it at the time. My father always thought your people were too strict with you.' She giggled lightly. 'All I can remember is you disappearing upstairs with Gordon Salter and then the next minute your folks storming in with Joel Hargreaves, demanding to know where you were.' She rolled her eyes and grinned. 'Funny how seeing someone you haven't seen in a while brings back old memories. You didn't come back to school with the rest of us after that summer holiday did you? Your folks sent you off to boarding school didn't they?'

'Yes.'

Lissa looked down at her coffee cup, gripping her hands together under the table to stop them from shaking.

Helen was looking at her watch. 'Heavens I must fly,' she exclaimed. 'I promised Bill I'd meet him in the DIY centre at one, and it's nearly that now. Come on poppet,' she commanded, picking up her son. 'Nice to see you again Lissa . . . Bye.'

She had been gone five minutes before Lissa felt relaxed enough to pick up her coffee cup and drink what was left of her coffee, and then when that was done she simply sat staring into space, unable to drag herself back to the present . . . too caught up in the memories of the past Helen had unleashed. What Helen remembered as merely an awkward incident had had such far reaching effects on her own life that even now still affected her.

Sighing faintly Lissa leaned back in her chair, willing her body to relax. She had been so excited about that party. Her parents had forbidden her to go, because they didn't approve of her crowd of friends. Why couldn't she have 'nice' friends like Amanda, her mother had constantly harped? Not that there was anything wrong with the crowd she went around with; they simply did not have the sort of moneyed background her parents approved of. This particular Saturday her parents had been dining with John's family. John and Amanda had been on the point of announcing their engagement, and Lissa had spent the afternoon at Helen's bewailing the fact that she was forbidden to attend Gordon's birthday party. Gordon Salter was something of a local Romeo, and Lissa had had a mammoth crush on him for several weeks. 'Why not go to the party anyway,' Helen had urged her. Her parents need never know. She could leave early and be back before they even knew she had been out. Even though she knew it was wrong, Lissa had agreed. After all what did her parents really care about her, she had argued rebelliously with herself. Amanda was the one they loved not her.

It had been surprisingly easy to deceive her parents. They had left home with Amanda a good hour before the party was due to start, leaving Lissa plenty of time to get ready. She didn't have many 'going out' clothes of her own, and on a reckless impulse she had raided her sister's wardrobe, 'borrowing' a mini dress which was rather shorter than short on her much taller frame. Make-up had come next. Some of Amanda's eyeshadow, and thick black liner applied with a rather unsteady hand. Lissa had thought the effect rather daring.

She had arranged to meet Helen at Gordon's house, but when she arrived there her friend had been busy talking to several people she did not know, and feeling suddenly shy she had felt reluctant to intrude. Gordon himself had materialised from the kitchen, and had greeted her with a brief kiss on the cheek. She had been so thrilled and excited that later she could barely remember accepting the drink he had given her, or drinking it. She must have done so though; and she had compounded her folly by drinking two more glasses of Gordon's special punch. That was why she had agreed to go upstairs with him, thrilled out of her mind that he should actually find her desirable. She hadn't been drunk, but what she had had to drink had been sufficient to rid her of her normally stifling inhibitions. She could remember quite vividly the thrills of excitement that had run up and down her spine when Gordon kissed her—boyish, quite inexperienced kisses really. They had been lying together on his bed, doing nothing more than exchanging explorative kisses when the door had suddenly been thrust open and a man Lissa didn't recognise had appeared framed darkly against the light behind him. Even now she shuddered slightly remembering the sickness and fear that had then crawled down her spine. Before she could even move her father was in the room, dragging her off the bed, saying things to her, calling her names ... that had numbed her senses and her tongue.

What had followed had all the trappings of the very worst kind of nightmares. Her parents had dragged her home in a thick silence, but once there, the real torment had started. What had she been doing with that boy? her mother demanded. They had questioned her in her father's study with Joel Hargreaves standing impassively by, listening to every single word. Lissa thought now she had never hated anyone in all her life as she had hated him that night. Send him away, she had demanded tearfully of her parents, but her father had refused. 'No Lissa. I want Joel to know what sort of girl his brother is going to get for a sister-in-law. Had you no thought for your sister when you disobeyed us?' he demanded, adding, 'do you think it fair that she should be tarred with the same brush as you?'

They had questioned her about what she had been doing with Gordon and in vain she had told them they had simply been kissing, blushing bright painful red to admit as much, but they had refused to believe her, saying why should they when she had already deceived them once by attending the party in the first place, and all the time Joel Hargreaves' watchful eyes had been on her, deriding . . . scorning . . . making her feel dirty and humiliated.

And her humiliation had not ended there. There had been a visit to their doctor; an examination which had left her racked with anguish and mental agony; and then she had been sent away to school. So that Amanda wouldn't have to bear the disgrace of a promiscuous younger sister, her parents had said.

It had taken years for Lissa to accept that she was not what her parents had called her; but the events of that night and the days which had followed had left her permanently scarred. To allow a man to so much as touch her was to relive again all that anguish; to endure the biting contempt in Joel Hargreaves' eyes when he looked down at her lying on the narrow bed with Gordon, her brief dress exposing all the long length of her legs, her mouth swollen from Gordon's kisses, all her tender, vulnerable adolescent emotions exposed to the cruel scrutiny of his worldliness.

'If you've finished with the table . . .'

It was several seconds before Lissa realised the waitress was speaking to her and that people were waiting for her to vacate her table. Almost stumbling she got to her feet and hurried out into the bitter February afternoon. Strange how fate worked. If she hadn't been such a coward about facing Joel she would never have come into the café, and then she would never have bumped into Helen; never have revived all those memories she had sought so firmly to conceal. She was literally shaking with reaction as she unlocked her car and a small moan broke from her mouth. Would it never end? Would she ever be able to put the past fully behind her and enter into a normal relationship with a man? Would she ever be able to take and give physical pleasure without the ever-present crushing guilt and self-disgust she now suffered from.

Why it was Joel Hargreaves whose face she saw every time another man touched her and not her father's she wasn't really sure. Her father had been the one to condemn her; to insist that she was lying . . . but it was the memory of Joel Hargreaves that brought her out in a cold sweat and turned her sleep into horrendous nightmares. Simon had been exultant when he accidentally hit on the fact that she was still a virgin, but he wouldn't be exultant if he knew why. He thought she was clinging to some silly out-moded convention of purity, whereas she knew the truth . . . that those cataclysmic events during her fifteenth summer had frozen and destroyed some essential female part of her; the pain of her humiliation so intense that it prevented her from allowing herself to feel anything sexual for any man.

By the time she drove through the gates of Winterly, Lissa had regained control of herself. As she stepped out of her Mini and walked towards the main door with long-legged grace no one could guess at the torment of emotional agony she had just endured, least of all the man watching her.

Joel's mouth twisted sardonically as he looked at her. She reminded him of a glossy, elegant chestnut filly he had once owned. There was pride and beauty in every movement of her graceful body, and also a wariness that warned him that she had come prepared to do battle if necessary.

Joel Hargreaves wasn't used to women keeping him at a distance; very much the opposite. What would have intrigued him in another woman, in Lissa grated on his nerves. He had known her since she was a teenager, and throughout all the years since she had treated him as though he were some vilely contaminated life-form.

He had once tried to talk to Amanda about it, but his sister-in-law had simply shrugged and said that Lissa was an odd girl.

Odd maybe ... beautiful and extremely desirable, yes. In the past she had never allowed him to get close enough to know her, but now, dramatically the situation had changed. Telling himself that he was a fool for even thinking of resurrecting what should have been no more than a passing whim he went to let her in.

'Lissa. You decided to come then.'

Lissa inclined her head coolly, praying that she had herself well under control. She was consumed by a wholly unfamiliar and extremely dangerous desire to give vent to the turmoil of feelings bubbling up inside her; to rave and scream at him that he and he alone was solely responsible for the destruction of her femininity . . . that she hated . . . hated and loathed him and that nothing . . . nothing would induce her to stay in his house.

As she followed him inside Joel caught the brilliant gleam of her eyes, and wondered if her anger was because she had had to leave her boyfriend for a weekend. Joel knew all about Simon Greaves. A very personable and persuasive young man.

'I think we'll talk in my study.'

Trust Joel to choose to do battle on his own home ground Lissa thought bitterly as he held the door open for her to precede him. She had visited Winterly on several occasions both when his parents lived there and since they had left, but this was the first time she had been in this particular room. The austerity of its furnishings were initially deceptive until one became aware of the intrinsic beauty of the antique desk and the silken beauty of the Aubusson rug covering the floor. A small display cabinet caught her eye and she held her breath for a moment awed by the collection of jade inside it.

'You like jade?'

Joel was watching her, and for once she saw no reason to conceal the truth from him.

'I love it,' she admitted.

'So do I. I started collecting it several years ago on a trip to Hong Kong.' He moved towards the case and then stopped abruptly as the study door opened and a harassed looking middle-aged woman burst in.

'Mr Hargreaves,' she began without preamble. 'I simply cannot have those children in my kitchen.

The moment my back's turned they're into my cupboards, upsetting everything . . .'

She paused to take a break and Joel inserted smoothly, 'Don't worry about it, Mrs Johnson. I'll soon have everything sorted out.'

'Well I certainly hope so.' Mrs Johnson seemed far from mollified and Lissa fought hard not to burst into impetuous speech and remind the older woman that if the children were being naughty it might possibly be remembered that they had only recently lost their parents and both sets of grandparents.

'If you'll just keep an eye on them for me while Miss Grant and I finish talking,' Joel continued, to his housekeeper. 'I promise you I'll take them off your hands.'

She withdrew but with bad grace, muttering something under her breath about not being paid to look after children. When she had gone Lissa raised her eyebrows and said coolly, '*That* is what you consider doing the best you can for the girls is it?'

She was surprised by the faint flush of colour staining his skin. 'In the past few days I've been trying to get a nanny. I haven't had much success.' He drummed impatiently on his desk for several seconds and then turned to face her, admitting, 'All the more reputable agencies are rather dubious about the fact that I'm a single man, and as for the rest.' His grim expression startled her a little. 'Well let's just say I'm not too keen on the idea of adding an eighteen year old au pair to my other problems.'

Lissa knew she should have felt triumphant, but the emotion uppermost in her heart was pity and concern for the children. She had experienced too much trauma and heartache during her own childhood, to treat the miseries of any other child's lightly.

'When can I see the girls, Joel?' she asked huskily.

'Soon . . . When we've finished talking.'

'How are they?'

How she hated having to ask him for anything, even something so mundane as information about her nieces, and she knew it showed in her voice from the twisted smile he gave her, his eyes glinting dark gold as he turned to look at her.

'Poor Lissa,' he mocked watching her. 'Forced to actually ask me for something. How that must hurt. Why are you so frightened of me Lissa?'

'I'm not.' Her chin firmed and she stared back at him. 'I simply don't like you very much that's all.'

He laughed then, the warm rich sound startling her. What could she possibly have said to make him laugh? It was obvious that he wasn't going to tell, so she insisted coolly, 'The girls, Joel. How are they coping?'

'On the surface, quite well,' he told her. 'Louise of course being older is finding it harder to accept that they're gone. Emma . . . well I can barely understand a word she says as it is. Louise seems to be able to interpret her chatter all right though. They've been asking for you,' he added abruptly. 'I didn't realise they knew you so well.'

'I've spent quite a lot of time with them.' It was true. She had looked after them for the odd weekend for her sister. Amanda knowing how much she loved children, and not being overly maternal herself had been delighted to leave them in her care.

'You really care about them don't you?' he said curtly, further surprising her.

Instantly she was defensive, glaring at him from angry emerald eyes as she responded bitterly, 'Why should that be so surprising? I happen to like children . . . I always have done.'

'And yet you've never given any indication that you'd like to get married and have your own,' Joel put in softly, 'I wonder why?'

Lissa had to turn away from him so that he couldn't read her expression. Her heart was thumping frantically, her pulse beat rocketing way out of control.

'Perhaps I just haven't met the right man yet,' she told him flippantly, hoping he wouldn't guess at her emotional turmoil. How could she ever have children of her own, feeling as she did about sex? It wasn't only the ability to love as a woman he had robbed her of, she thought, hating him, it was also the ability to mother children . . . And now he even wanted to take her nieces away from her.

'I'm not prepared to give up the girls, Joel,' she told him, pivoting round to face him. 'Amanda left them in my care . . . and I don't care what you say,' she cried out passionately, 'I can't really believe that any caring judge would rule that the care of strangers—because that's what your nanny will be—will be more beneficial, even with all the material advantages you can give them, than my love. You *don't* love them Joel . . . not the way I do.' She was close to tears and had to blink them away, horrified when she opened her eyes again to find that he was looming over her, the gold speckles in his eyes igniting with fierce heat.

'Like hell I don't,' he told her thickly. 'You seem to have conveniently forgotten that their father was my brother . . . I only want what is best for them Lissa . . .'

'No, you don't. You just want to take them away from me.'

Her voice was high and strained, hysteria edging in under her self-control. She could see Joel looking at her, and she could feel his anger.

'Don't be such a bloody fool,' he flung at her. 'You seem to be developing a persecution complex where I'm concerned, Lissa. Oh yes,' he gritted grimly watching her with cold eyes. 'I'm well aware of the extraordinary lengths you go to avoid my company. I know quite well that Amanda had strict instructions never to invite you to the house when there was any chance that I might be around. Just what have I ever done to warrant such antipathy Lissa. Tell me?'

She shrugged lightly, struggling for self-control. It seemed impossible that the events that were burned so painfully into her memory should not exist for him. But perhaps it was safer for her that he did not remember, she told herself, her nerve endings jumping tensely when the next minute, he said with silky softness, 'Or can I guess? Does all this haughty disdain you exhibit towards me spring from the fact that I once caught you in bed with your boyfriend?'

The brilliant wave of scarlet flooding her skin gave her away, and she watched his mouth twist in wry mockery, hating him with all the intense passion of her nature when he drawled tauntingly,

'You should be grateful that you were stopped when you were. A teenage pregnancy is no fun . . .'

God, how she hated him, Lissa thought feeling the nauseous loathing rise up inside her. She wanted to scream and cry . . . to tear that smooth smile from his face with her nails. She hated him . . . hated him . . . Her attention was deflected from her own inner turmoil when she heard Joel saying calmly, 'No Lissa, I don't think the best thing for the girls is for them to be constantly shuttled between us, as though we were divorced parents. Children, especially children such as Louise and Emma who have already suffered the loss of their parents, need security and stability, and in an attempt to give them both, I've decided that what I need is not a nanny, but a wife.'

Lissa could only stare at him, but hard on the heels of her shock came the knowledge that if he did marry, she would lose her nieces, because surely a judge was bound to favour the suit of a man who had not only wealth but also a wife, above the claims of a girl, struggling alone on a little more than adequate salary.

'No comment?' she heard Joel saying, the words reaching her through a fog of thoughts. 'You don't want to know the identity of my wife-to-be?'

'Why should I?' Lissa managed to croak the denial. 'It's nothing to do with me?'

'On the contrary,' Joel assured her with smooth silkiness. 'It has everything to do with you my dear. You see, I've decided that the very best solution to Louise and Emma's problem would be for you and I to marry thus uniting both their guardians and providing them with a stable background.'

Lissa barely heard his last words. 'You and I . . .?' She stared at him, the colour leaving her face on an ebb tide of shock. 'No, I . . .'

'Lissa, neither of us are foolish teenagers any longer.'

'We don't love one another . . . we don't even like one another,' Lissa interrupted harshly. 'How can you even think of a marriage between us?'

'Oh quite easily.' He was smiling at her in a way that told her that little though he might like her, he found the shape of her sexually desirable. Shock hit her on a tidal wave, swamping her. Joel desired *her*.

'You see,' he mocked her softly, 'we could have a lot more in common than you think. There is no need for our marriage to be a sterile one Lissa. On the contrary . . .'

Lissa felt as though she were drowning in some whirlpool far too frenzied for her to fight. 'But you've always avoided marriage,' she whispered huskily, 'I remember Amanda once saying that she thought you'd never marry.'

'At one time I thought that myself,' he agreed laconically, 'but that was before John died.'

'And if I refuse . . .?' What did she mean 'if'. Of course she was going to refuse . . . but a thought had taken possession of her brain . . . the seed of an idea, that at last she might have found a way to make Joel pay for all the agony and shame he had caused her.

'Then I'll have to look around for someone else,' he told her calmly. 'Make no mistake about it Lissa. For the girls' sake I intend to marry. I should prefer that my wife is you, but if you refuse, then I shall simply marry someone else.'

'And I'll lose the girls.' She breathed the words softly, but he heard them and shrugged.

'The choice is yours. I'm not, after all, asking you to make any sacrifice I'm not prepared to make myself. We'll both be giving up our freedom . . . and one thing more Lissa.' He came towards her standing only feet away, but making no move to reach out and touch her. She felt almost suffocated by his proximity but refused to step back, making herself endure it. 'Our marriage will not be an empty legal bond only, but very real, in every sense of the word.'

'But I don't want you.' She said it through stiff lips forcing them to frame the words, half of her praying that he would take back his proposal; and the other half, the bitter, angry half hoping that he would not.

'How can you know that,' he taunted softly. 'We haven't been lovers yet.'

Nor ever will be, the bitter half of her exulted. Let him marry her . . . let him think he was going to have it all his own way, but when she lay in his bed and in his arms she would be as cold as ice; as devoid of the ability to give and take pleasure as she had always been, since he had destroyed the feminine core of her. Ignoring all the urgings of common sense Lissa faced him, praying that he wouldn't see the bitterness in her eyes, and that he wouldn't guess exactly why she was marrying him. He was using her affection for the girls to force her into this marriage . . . a marriage she was sure that would not stop him continuing with his many affairs, but what he did not know was that she was also going to use him . . . as the instrument of her revenge.

'Very well Joel . . . I agree to marry you.'

She was surprised to see the heated flicker of triumph burn dark gold in his eyes. He took a step towards her and she backed away, but before either of them could speak the door burst open and the elder of their nieces came rushing in.

'Auntie Lissa . . . Auntie Lissa . . . I heard you talking.' The petite four year old ran up to Lissa, clinging tightly to her legs, the blonde head buried in her skirt. 'Are you going to stay here for ever,' Louise demanded when Lissa bent down to pick her up. 'I want you to . . . so does Emma . . .'

'Yes, Louise, she's going to stay here for ever,' Lissa heard Joel saying from a distance, and just for a moment she felt a twinge of apprehension at the deep note of triumph in his voice, but then she banished it, telling herself she was imagining things. She was the one who should be feeling triumphant. She had got her nieces, and she had also got the means of repaying Joel for all the years of anguish and pain he had caused her. He might think their marriage was going to be a 'normal' one, but she knew different.

CHAPTER THREE

LISSA woke up the next morning feeling totally disorientated; initially by the strangeness of her room, and then by the huge weight of depression which seemed to have descended upon her out of nowhere. And then she remembered.

She had agreed to marry Joel! She closed her eyes and groaned, her head falling back against her pillow. How could she have been so stupid? She would have to tell him she had changed her mind. It was her own silly temper and pride that had led into folly; the old burning anger cum anguish she always experienced whenever she was with him. Why oh why after all these years, should Joel still be the one whose contempt and rejection of her hurt so badly? Was it because he had been the one to thrust open that bedroom door and see her? Was it because somehow in her innermost mind she had because of that confused him in some way with her father? They were questions Lissa could not answer; all she did know was that whenever she came in contact with him she was reminded of the way he had looked at her that night . . . and how for one weak minute she had longed to cry out to him to understand and forgive her . . . Shivering faintly despite the centrally heated warmth of her bedroom, she was just contemplating how best to tell him that she had changed her mind and that she was certainly not prepared to marry him; even for the sake of her nieces when the door burst open and the two little girls rushed in, both still in their nightdresses.

Louise reached her first, flinging herself on to the bed and cuddling up next to her. Emma, still very much a toddler needed a helping hand, but there was no mistaking the enthusiasm in her hug when she was finally on the bed with Lissa and her sister.

'You're going to marry Uncle Joel and then you'll be our new mummy and daddy,' Louise announced importantly.

Lissa's heart sank. She felt trapped and desperate. How could she have been so crazy as to allow those old hurts to trap her into her present position. It seemed mediaeval and archaic now, in the cold clear light of a February morning that she should actually have contemplated marrying Joel, simply to even punish him for the pain he had once caused her. That was all over and done with now. But Joel . . . why did he want to marry her?

That was simple Lissa told herself; he wanted someone to look after the children who was not going to walk out on him. If she backed out she would lose the girls, Lissa reminded herself, looking at the two blonde heads, nestled together against her warmth. As she watched them, a melting, aching wave of love for them suffused her. If she didn't marry Joel, he would find someone who would and the girls would be lost to her for ever. Could she endure that? Looking at them Lissa knew she could not. This deeply maternal feeling she felt towards them was something she had always kept well hidden from others. Only Amanda had been aware of it, wryly amused by her sister's passionate love for her daughters, warning Lissa that when she married she would soon discover the drawbacks to being a mother. 'You want them because this way you can satisfy your mothering instincts without having to endure someone's lovemaking', an inner voice warned her, but Lissa refused to listen, her fingers curling slightly into the bedclothes as she tried to deny the thoughts. Whose fault was it that she froze every time a man touched her she asked herself, trying to whip up some of the anger she had that had consumed her last night. Not hers!

Her bedroom door opened again, and she blinked in stunned disbelief as Joel strolled in carrying a breakfast tray, which he put down on the table by the bed.

'Who said you two could come in here?' he demanded of the girls, ruffling the blonde curls and drawing stifled giggles from Louise.

'You and Lissa are going to be our new mummy and daddy, aren't you?' Louise demanded importantly of him, and yet Lissa could see that beyond the child's self-importance was a shadow of uncertainty and fear, and all her inner arguments against what they were doing melted. If for no other reason surely the sacrifice demanded of her was not too great when she thought of what it would mean to the girls. Joel was right; they needed the security and stability of a proper family unit, and if she didn't marry him, Joel would stand by his threat to find someone who would. She loved them too much to let someone else take her place with them, Lissa knew, and as she raised stormy hazel eyes to meet the mocking gold of Joel's, she knew that he had faithfully monitored each and every single thought that had passed through her head since he walked in the room.

'Too late for second thoughts,' he mouthed softly. There were two cups on the tray, Lissa noticed for the first time, and she gaped a little as Joel promptly started to fill them both with aromatic freshly brewed coffee. No doubt he was used to providing breakfast in bed for his legion of girlfriends, she thought waspishly, but he had no right to look so at ease and relaxed as he did so. He was dressed casually in jeans and a soft woollen checked shirt.

'Mrs Johnson's day off,' he explained laconically, handing her a cup.

'Very impressive,' Lissa responded tautly. 'But then I expect you've had plenty of practice.'

She saw his mouth tighten, the good humour that had lightened his eyes going, and a certain hard coldness taking its place. 'I thought we'd agreed to bury our differences and start afresh,' he said curtly. 'Two adults who spend all their time together back-biting at one another aren't going to help these two.'

Lissa knew he was right, and she bit her lower lip in mortification, hating him for putting her in the wrong and for making her appear selfish. She ought to be thinking of the girls and not herself. Joel obviously had. There were two beakers on the tray and he poured orange juice into each of them, handing them to his nieces. He was rewarded with a beaming smile from Emma, and a small frown from Louise, who confided artlessly, 'When Daddy makes Mummy's breakfast for her, he always gets back into bed with her. Sometimes he tells Nanny to come and take us away,' she added importantly.

Lissa could feel the colour stealing up under her skin, but it was impossible for her to drag her eyes away from the amusement sparkling in Joel's.

'Blushing.' He ran a teasing finger along the curve of her cheek as he sat down on the edge of her bed. 'How novel, and why I wonder should the thought of married sex embarrass you when you yourself must surely be no stranger to the early morning rituals between lovers.'

Lissa wanted to vigorously deny what he was saying, but how could she without betraying the truth?

'I must go back to London today,' she mumbled, desperately anxious to change the subject. She was going hot and cold all over with the onset of a familiar fear. It seemed incredible and she knew that Joel would never have believed it, but the closest she had come to real intimacy with any man in the years since her fifteenth summer was what she was sharing with him right now. Suddenly she became intensely aware of the weight of his body on her mattress; the warm male scent of him as he leaned forward to tickle Louise. The little girl giggled and moved closer to her, grabbing the soft fabric of her nightdress. It was a fine lawn cotton, and covered her quite adequately, but as Louise grabbed the fabric she was suddenly intensely conscious of the way it was tightening across her breasts. She could feel Joel watching her as though his glance were burning into her skin.

'London?'

The sharpness in his voice made her tense, and when she managed to compose herself sufficiently to meet his eyes they were cold and angry.

'Joel, I'll have to arrange something about my house . . . and then there's Simon and my job. I'll have to explain that . . .'

'I'll do all the explaining necessary,' he told her curtly. 'I want you to stay here with the girls.'

'But Simon . . .' Lissa expostulated. 'I must tell him myself that . . .'

'That you won't be sharing his bed any longer?' Joel bit out grimly. 'That he'll be losing a lover as well as a secretary. No Lissa, I'll tell him for you. I don't want you seeing him again, now that you've agreed to marry me. I suppose it hasn't occurred to you that if he'd really thought anything of you, he'd have proposed marriage . . . knowing how you feel about the girls.'

It was on the tip of Lissa's tongue to tell him that Simon had, but for some reason she suppressed the words. 'What are you so afraid of Joel?' she lashed out instead. 'That if I see Simon I won't be able to resist jumping straight into bed with him. You always did have a high opinion of me didn't you?' she finished sarcastically, watching the way his mouth twisted with bitter derision as he looked at her, and wondering why she should feel this knife twist of pain so deep inside herself; why she should lash herself so unmercifully, when she knew . . . oh how she knew exactly how much he despised her. Why should she seek further confirmation of that knowledge so determinedly?

'You've certainly never gone out of your way to show yourself to me in a good light have you?' Joel countered. 'In fact I sometimes think you deliberately want me to think the worst of you Lissa. I've often wondered why?'

He got up before she could make any retort,

dropping light kisses on the two small blonde heads of his nieces as he did so.

'Aren't you going to kiss Lissa too?' Louise piped up instantly. 'Daddy always kissed Mummy before he went to work.'

'But I'm not going to work,' Joel explained, ruffling her curls. 'I'm going downstairs to make some telephone calls. However, poppet, just to please you.' He bent his head, and although Lissa cringed back as far as she could, until the back of her head was pressed against the unyielding brass of the Victorian bedstead, it didn't stop Joel from kissing her, the torment of the warmth of his mouth moving softly against her own making her shiver with shock and fear. When he released her he was frowning and Lissa held her breath, wondering if she had betrayed herself, and if he was now having second thoughts about marrying her. He was a virile man; even she could see that and when he discovered that ... that she was neither prepared nor able to be a true wife to him. Tell him, tell him the truth now an inner voice cautioned ... but she couldn't ... she couldn't lay herself open to the male mockery and contempt she would see in his eyes if she did. And besides she would lose the girls. No, after they were married ... after they were married she would tell him that she had changed her mind and that she could not accept him as her lover. After all he would still have what he wanted from her; the children and her service as a stand-in mother. For the rest ... well she doubted that he had had any thoughts of being faithful to her in any case ... Feeling a little uncomfortable because she knew she was deceiving him, Lissa was glad when he turned his back on her and walked towards the door. Once he was through it and had closed it behind him she let out a shaky breath. Emma took her thumb out of her mouth and stared up at her with golden brown eyes. A huge smile split her solemn little face and she said firmly, 'Mummy.'

Lissa had to dash away tears. Amanda had complained that Emma was slow to speak because she had Louise to translate for her, and it seemed prophetic that she should choose now of all times to start.

'No, not Mummy,' Louise corrected her sister, 'Auntie Lissa . . . but you can call her Mummy I s'pose,' she said kindly. 'Shall I call you Mummy too . . . and Uncle Joel, Daddy?' she asked Lissa.

'You must call us whatever you like Louise,' Lissa told her. She suspected that by the time she reached school age Emma would not be able to remember her parents, but Louise was old enough to do so and the last thing Lissa wanted to do was to try to erase from her memory the reality of her parents. The best thing to do was to let Louise feel free to decide for herself and see what happened, she decided, trying to occupy her mind with the girls' problems and not her own.

She left them playing together on the bed while she showered and dressed, and then wearing comfortable jeans and a soft russet silk shirt that toned with her hair, she shepherded them back to their own room.

Joel had put them in his own and John's old nursery, and while the bedroom with its bathroom and study-sitting room was large and airy the decor was more suited to two teenage boys rather than two small girls. Making a mental note to talk to him about it, and to ask him about the girls' toys and clothes, Lissa helped them to get dressed and took them downstairs.

The sooner a proper routine was established, the sooner they would overcome the trauma of their parents' death. Making another mental note to enquire locally about play groups, Lissa headed for the kitchen, suddenly conscious that Louise was hanging back, a worried frown puckering her forehead.

'Come on darling, you want some breakfast, don't you?' Lissa asked gently.

'Mrs Johnson doesn't like us going in the kitchen,' was Louise's quavery response. 'She says we're pests and that it's time Uncle Joel made some proper arrangements for us.'

Listening to this artless confirmation that little pitchers did indeed have long ears, Lissa repressed a quiver of anger against the housekeeper. Surely the older woman could have made allowances, knowing the circumstances surrounding the girls.

'Uncle Joel got us a new nanny,' Louise continued confidingly, 'because Nanny Jo's boyfriend didn't want her to come and live here with us, but we didn't like our new nanny . . .'

Lissa was not surprised that 'Nanny' Jo's boyfriend was reluctant to allow his girlfriend to live virtually alone with a man of Joel's calibre, even she was aware of his powerful, vibrant brand of masculinity, but while other women were attracted by it, she was repelled, she told herself, witness her revulsion when Joel had kissed her. And yet there had been no violence, no domination in his kiss . . . If anything the first touch of his mouth against her own had been almost tender, coaxing . . . Shutting such dangerous thoughts away Lissa turned her attention to the task of getting the girls' breakfast, secretly appalled to discover how little there was in the way of food in the kitchen cupboards. She was going to have to speak to Joel about his housekeeper and she grimaced faintly at the thought.

She had just settled the girls at the comfortable farmhouse table with plates of toast and honey, when Joel walked in.

'Any chance of a cup of coffee?' he enquired of Lissa, lifting one eyebrow interrogatively. When she nodded assent, he sat down between the two girls, deftly preventing Emma from dropping her toast sticky side down on to her lap. Watching his easy confidence with the girls, Lissa realised she was seeing a new side of him. In her mind he was and always had been the sardonic contemptuous enemy of her youth; the man who had torn from her all her romantic yearnings and dreams and tossed them back to her blemished and made sordid by his totally unexpected intrusion into the bedroom where she had been experiencing her first tentative and innocent forays into the land of sensual pleasure. Had they been left alone she knew that nothing more than a few fumbling kisses and caresses would have been exchanged between Gordon and herself. For all his image as the school pin-up, his worldly experience had not been more than hers, and with the wisdom of age she realised that both of them would have drawn back before they had gone much further, but the reaction of her father and the disapproval of Joel, the stranger he had brought with him to witness her shame and degradation, had made it seem as though she were more of a nymphomaniac than a shy and rather naïve fifteen year old experiencing virtually her first kiss. Now she could accept that her parents had been over-strict with her, much more so than they had been with Amanda, but Amanda had been the image of her mother while she apparently, or so Amanda had once confided, was very much like their father's sister ... someone who was never mentioned at home, and who apparently as a teenager during the War had led a rather promiscuous life, eventually leaving home and disappearing. This explained some of her parents' strictness and even possibly her father's dislike of her, Lissa acknowledged, but surely if they had loved her as they undoubtedly loved Amanda they would have seen—known—that she was not the wanton creature they themselves had branded her.

She could still vividly recall her shock and mental anguish at discovering from another of the pupils that the school she had been sent to was for 'naughty' girls. 'What have you done to get here,' the latter had asked her.' Boasting, 'I'm here because I hate my new step-brother.'

The nuns hadn't been actively unkind, indeed some of them showed an extremely enlightened attitude towards their wayward pupils, but Lissa had felt too out of step ... too alien to respond to them. She had also felt besmirched ... dirty and degraded ... defiled in a way that made her recoil from any human contact.

'Lissa?'

She came back to reality with a start, uncomfortably conscious of the strange look in

Joel's eyes as he looked at her. 'Where on earth have you been?' he asked softly.

Just for a moment the concern she heard in his voice touched her and she said huskily, 'To hell . . .' bitterly regretting her weakness when she saw first shock and then caution enter his eyes.

'It's too late now for backing out,' he told her harshly, revealing that he had totally misunderstood her comment. 'I've already spoken to Greaves and told him that you're marrying me.'

How possessive he sounded, Lissa thought wryly, almost as though telling Simon they were to marry had given him a great deal of pleasure. 'I've also spoken to our local vicar.' He saw her start of surprise and smiled grimly. 'What were you expecting Lissa—a civil ceremony.' He shook his head. 'My grandparents, my parents and John were all married in our local church. We won't have a large wedding of course . . . in fact I've arranged a very quiet ceremony; just the Vicar and a handful of witnesses. His wife has offered to have the girls for the afternoon. I've given out that we'd planned to announce our engagement on your birthday, but that because of what has happened, we've brought the wedding forward for the sake of the children.'

Her birthday was six weeks away, and Lissa marvelled at Joel's ability to remember such a trivial thing, just as she was chilled by his ability to reason and plan. It made sense of course—she was the last person to want a lot of speculation and curiosity about why they were marrying.

'And Lissa one thing more,' he continued in a quiet voice. 'Once we *are* married I shall expect you to stay faithful to your vows. We live in a very quiet village and . . .'

'. . . and a front of respectability must be maintained at all times,' she finished bitterly for him, remembering that this had been her parents' attitude. Almost as though he read her mind, Joel put in curtly, 'You hurt your parents very deeply with your unconventional behaviour Lissa, but I won't accept it the way they did.'

'Hurt *them*!' Lissa was incredulous . . . struck dumb by his arrogant claim. He knew nothing about her relationship with her family, nothing at all . . .

'Yes.' Joel continued as though she hadn't interrupted. 'I can vividly remember your father's shock that night when you deceived him to go to that party. They were dining with my parents and your father developed a migraine. I offered to run them back as your mother couldn't drive. When they got home and found you gone your father was beside himself. Luckily your mother remembered the telphone number of your friend and it was from her parents that they learned where you were . . . Your mother explained to me later the problems they'd had with you . . . how wild and uncontrollable you were, how you'd got in with a bad set . . . I must say at first I was disinclined to believe them, but when I walked into that house with your father and found half the kids in it were put of their minds on drugs and the other half on drink . . .'

Lissa could have told him that the drugs had come from the older brother of one of the boys there who had brought them home from university, and as for the drink . . . well most of them had been so young and inexperienced that a couple of glasses of wine had been more than sufficient to go to their heads, never mind the weird punch concoction that had been served.

'But of course you were out for another kind of thrill weren't you Lissa . . .? How many others had you been to bed with before him?'

'Does it matter?' She felt literally sick, her body shaking with tension as she saw herself through Joel's eyes. She remembered how the brief dress had ridden up exposing her thighs, the low neckline revealing the curves of her breasts and she shuddered deeply. To bolster herself up she demanded huskily, 'If you disapprove of me so much Joel, why marry me? If I've slipped so far beyond the pale, I'm surprised you're even contemplating it. My morals . . .'

'It isn't your morals that are at issue,' Joel cut in angrily. 'I don't give a damn how many men you've slept with Lissa. I'm not hypocritical enough to expect a woman to remain chaste while a man does not . . . no, what baffles me is that you should have so little respect for yourself . . . so little self-pride. The gift of your body to another human being is exactly that—a gift—not something to be thrown away lightly, but something to be treasured . . .'

'And to ensure that Emma and Louise treasure theirs, are you going to keep a ball and chain on them while they're growing up, as my father did me,' Lissa hit out blindly.

Joel looked at her, his expression hard to define, but somewhere in it was a pity that lashed at her pride, and made her burn with resentment. How dare he pity her. How dare he falsely accuse her . . . force her into a set pattern that was not hers and never had been.

'No . . . I shall tell them that whatever they do in life is by their own choice, and it matters little what it is, or what others think, as long as they can face themselves and keep their own self-respect intact. Self-respect is more important than the opinions of others; than momentary sexual release . . .'

'And you of course are speaking from experience,' Lissa taunted bitterly.

'I've never made love to a woman I don't both like and honour, if that's what you mean,' Joel agreed with devastating candour.

A bitter smile curved Lissa's mouth. 'Then obviously you're prepared to make an exception in my case.' She could feel tears pricking the backs of her eyes, and hated herself for her weakness. Flinging down the cloth she was holding, she hurried out of the kitchen, conscious of Joel calling her name, but the strident shrill of the telephone prevented him from following her.

It was half an hour or so before she felt able to go back downstairs.

The girls were seated at the now cleared kitchen table, busily drawing on large sheets of paper. Joel was filling the coffee maker and turned as she walked in.

'Let's just put the past behind us Lissa,' he said in a clipped voice, without looking at her. 'All I want is your promise that you will adhere to our marriage vows; that there'll be no sneaking off to meet the likes of Greaves.'

Was he worried that she might neglect the children? That must be it, Lissa thought subduing a mild bout of hysteria at the thought of her of all people sneaking off to meet any man. If only he knew! But he must not know! Quite why she should feel so strongly that she must keep the truth from him Lissa wasn't sure. She had sensed a compassion and gentleness in his attitude towards the girls that she had once believed alien to his nature and if he knew the truth that compassion might even be extended to include herself. But she didn't want his compassion, she told herself angrily. She didn't *want* to like him . . . she didn't want him to like her. To stop herself from pursuing this potentially dangerous line of thought she asked sweetly, 'And you Joel, do you intend to keep to your vows?'

'Do you want me to?'

He was challenging her, Lissa knew that, but her eyes dropped away from the golden gleam of his. He laughed softly, and feather light shivers of alarm coursed over her body as he came towards her. 'What an enigma you are Lissa,' he said quietly. 'What did I say to provoke this.' His fingers touched her heated face and she blushed harder, hating herself for doing so. 'Surely it can't be the thought of me as your lover that makes you so hot and bothered. After all to you what's one more man?'

'Auntie Lissa, come and look at my drawing,' Louise demanded, giving Lissa an opportune excuse for moving away. Her heart was thumping jerkily, her body a melting pot of strange and alien sensations, her nerves stretched like over-fine wire.

'I've got to go out,' Joel informed her. 'I'm interviewing several applicants for John's job.' A shadow crossed his face, and Lissa felt a tug of sympathy for him. He had been very close to his brother, she knew.

Originally Joel had overseen both the estate and the business, but after their father had retired John had taken over as Managing Director of the company, and Joel had concentrated on running the estate, bringing in many new innovative measures, according to Amanda, but he had also been on hand to help and advise John whenever his help was needed. He had other business interests too according to Amanda, with money invested wisely in a variety of enterprises. All in all he was a shrewd and very astute man; a husband many women would be delighted to have; physically he was extremely attractive, his manner towards the children was both gentle and firm. He would make an excellent father, she found herself thinking, swiftly denying the thought. There would be no children for them, and if he didn't like it well then ... he would ... he would simply have to divorce her ... She subdued a bubble of hysterical laughter forming in her throat. How many potential brides were thinking about divorce even before the wedding ceremony took place.

Later on in the day, when she had settled the girls for a nap, having previously taken them for a walk, Lissa had time on her hands to think. She should never have agreed to marry Joel she knew, but having agreed how could she back out now, without losing the girls? Already this one day spent with them had been full of so many small pleasures; had moved her to such love and laughter that she couldn't bear the thought of being without them. Joel wanted to marry her because she was their aunt, not because he cared in the slightest for her, she reminded herself, trying to make herself feel less guilty. That he had also intimated to her that he desired her physically, she tried to dismiss. How could he desire her when by his own admission all his previous women had had his respect and affection; neither of which there was the remotest chance of her having. She should really go to London and pack up her belongings, make arrangements for her flat, but Joel had told her that he would arrange to do all that was necessary. He wanted her to stay with the girls he had told her.

Sighing faintly Lissa tried not to think about the looming proximity of the wedding. Instead she turned her mind to working out how best to tell Joel that she thought he ought to find another housekeeper, one who had a more relaxed attitude towards children.

CHAPTER FOUR

'WHY aren't you wearing a white dress.' Louise scowled, looking uncannily like Joel, as she sat on Lissa's bed watching her dress. 'Brides always wear white dresses,' she complained. 'I've seen them!'

'Yes, darling I know,' Lissa agreed, 'but this isn't that sort of wedding. Now you're going to be a good girl for Mrs Chartwell aren't you? She's going to look after you and Emma while Uncle Joel and I get married.'

'She's got a dog,' Louise told her, instantly distracted, excited colour glowing in her cheeks. 'Can we have a dog Lissa? Mummy said we couldn't because granny was all . . . alle . . .'

'Allergic,' Lissa finished for her, remembering her mother's aversion for any kind of pet. 'We'll see,' she told the little girl, 'I'll have to ask Uncle Joel.'

'Ask Uncle Joel what?'

Lissa felt her stomach muscles tense as Joel walked into her room. He was already dressed for the ceremony in a dark pin-striped suit and a fine white silk shirt. He looked very tall and male, Lissa thought shakily, and for some reason she had the oddest desire to be held against his chest and comforted the way he had comforted Emma the other evening when she fell over and grazed her knee. She wanted her fears and miseries soothed away, the way he had soothed Emma's she thought crazily, stunned by the impact of her thoughts.

'If we can have a dog,' Louise replied promptly, forcing her to take notice of what she was saying, rather than abandoning herself to the enormity of her own thoughts.

'Louise would like a dog,' Lissa cut in shakily, 'I told her she must ask you.'

'I don't see why not . . . but . . . only if you're a very good girl,' Joel added cautioningly when Louise started to bounce up and down on the bed, 'and that includes not making Mrs Johnson angry.'

His mention of the housekeeper made Lissa remember her own doubts about the other woman, and saying firmly, 'Louise, be a good girl and go and see if Emma's awake will you?' she sent her out of earshot.

Joel was frowning as the door closed behind her and Lissa said quickly, 'I sent her away because I wanted to talk to you about Mrs Johnson. I don't like her attitude towards the girls—at least I don't like what I've seen of it. I realise that staff can be hard to find but . . .'

'If you want to replace her you can do so,' Joel surprised her by saying without argument. 'I've had a few doubts myself,' he told her grimly, 'but I've already been accused of spoiling the girls, so I held my peace.'

Spoiling them? By whom Lissa wondered.

'All ready?' His glance skimmed her pale face and then studied the soft cream wool of her suit. The colour was a perfect foil for the richness of her hair, and although Lissa thought she looked far too pale she was conscious of looking good in the outfit—a new one she had purchased for spring and so not yet worn. She had confined her hair in an elegant knot, and on impulse had driven into the nearest town the previous afternoon and managed to find an absurd concoction of feathers and net in a Princess Diana style which made her suit look much more bridal.

'Almost. I've just got to dress Emma and Louise.'

'I'll do that for you.'

Once again he had stunned her.

'Don't look like that,' he told her grimly. 'I do know how to. What's the matter Lissa?' he mocked. 'Surprised to discover that I'm not quite the ogre you thought?'

His perspicacity unnerved her. He saw far too much, far too clearly.

She managed a light shrug. 'It's just that I find it surprising that you should know so much about child care—you being a single man.'

Somehow she managed to make his caring sound suspect, and was instantly ashamed of herself, but he only said quietly, 'I don't find it at all unmanly Lissa, and if you do, then I'm very sorry for you . . . but it's your problem. John was a devoted father and spent a lot of time with the girls. Amanda had a nanny but both of them believed in being with the children as much as possible and I think that is the right attitude. Too many women shut their husbands out of their childrens' lives, especially when the children are very young.'

Once again he had made her feel very much in the wrong . . . very shallow and unfair in her attitudes, Biting her lip, she turned away from him and concentrated on putting on her lip gloss.

'Don't wear too much of that stuff,' he startled her by drawling, her eyes swivelled sharply to meet the amusement in his.

'I don't want to get it all over me when I kiss you,' he explained softly, apparently fascinated by the slow crawl of hot colour turning her pale skin pink. Her fingers went instinctively to her lips as though to protect them from even the suggestion of his touch. A thick sound stifled in the back of his throat drew her attention back to Joel. He was standing watching her, with an unreadable expression in his eyes, their gold darkened to a burning topaz.

'You've got all the tricks Lissa,' he told her bitterly, 'I'll give you that . . . but you're wasting your time playing the shy bride on me. I know the real you—remember . . .'

'And knowing—still want me,' she flung at him dangerously. For a moment the tension of his body frightened her and then he seemed to force himself to relax.

'An inexplicable weakness,' he agreed in a slow drawl, 'but one which I suspect time and familiarity will eliminate.'

He was gone before Lissa could retort. She stared into the mirror at her own baffled and furious expression. Had he really meant to intimate that once he had made love to her a few times he would no longer want her? No doubt about it! Her mouth compressed grimly. Oh, she hated him . . . hated him . . .

Angry colour sparkled in her eyes as she joined him downstairs, her cheeks still glowing faintly with the heat of her resentment. Both girls bounced excitedly around them as Joel shepherded them out to the car.

'Mrs Chartwell offered to have them for the night, but I didn't think that was a good idea,' Joel told her quietly as he opened the car doors. 'They've had bad dreams just about every night since their parents died, and I don't want to subject them to any unnecessary alterations in routine.'

Lissa managed a casual shrug. 'Well we're hardly a normal bride and groom are we,' she countered.

'What's normal?' Joel held open the car door for her and Lissa shivered remembering what he had said about their marriage. As he closed the car door on her she had a wild impusle to thrust it open and tell him that she couldn't go through with it. The words hovered on her lips, but just at that moment Louise leaned forward from the rear of the car and said happily. 'After today I'm going to call you "Mummy" Aunt Lissa, and I'm going to call Uncle Joel "Daddy", and we'll be together for always won't we? You'll never, ever go away to heaven and leave us will you?' The anxiety in the high childish voice silenced Lissa's tongue. How could she back out . . . how could she subject the girls to more upset and upheaval?

The answer was quite simply that she could not, and it was this and nothing else that kept her going through the brief, tense ceremony that made her Joel's wife. As he had threatened, once she was he bent his head to kiss her. The warmth of his breath fanning her face made her feel faint; but the acute nausea she was used to experiencing when men came so threateningly close to her never came; nor on this occasion was she attacked by those flashing pictures that so often in the past had tormented her; images of Joel staring down at her dishevelled clothing and flushed face, Joel disapproving and contemptuous . . . perhaps because this time it was Joel himself who was kissing her, Lissa thought numbly, keeping her mouth firmly closed as his lips moved over it. She could feel him checking slightly, anxiously aware of the narrowed scrutiny in his eyes as they searched hers. Her heart was thumping alarmingly.

'If you're thinking of reneging on our bargain Lissa, then don't,' he warned her softly.

There was no time for him to say anything more because they were being congratulated by the Vicar and Joel had to turn aside from her to respond to him.

An hour later having accepted the celebratory glass of sherry the vicar's wife had offered, and collected the girls, Lissa sank thankfully into the leather upholstery of Joel's Jaguar. She felt exhausted, both emotionally and physically; totally drained by the effort of maintaining a façade of calm, while inwardly she was a mass of nerves.

Joel too seemed unusually silent as he drove them back to Winterly; even the girls were a little subdued Lissa noticed. Now that the ceremony was over and they were actually man and wife she felt foolish wearing her frivolous hat and the first thing she did as she walked into the house was to take it off, halting with it still in her hands as she observed the determined expression of the housekeeper as she came into the hall. The grim look in the older woman's eyes, plus the fact that she was dressed in her outdoor clothes gave Lissa an inkling of what was to come, and she was proved right. The moment Joel was through the door Mrs Johnson announced curtly that she was leaving. As she made this pronouncement she eyed Lissa with disfavour, adding that she had told Joel when she took the job that single gentlemen were what she preferred working for and that she never worked in households where there were children.

Quickly shepherding the girls upstairs Lissa left Joel to deal with her alone. It was about ten minutes before she heard Mrs Johnson's small car drive away.

'Well I'm afraid it looks as though we're going to have to find a new housekeeper a little earlier than we'd planned,' Joel announced as he walked into the nursery. 'I did try to persuade her to stay on long enough to give you time to adjust, but she wouldn't agree.' He looked rather grim and Lissa wondered if he considered her incapable of looking after the four of them herself. At the convent the girls had had to look after their own rooms, and they had also had to take turns working in the kitchens. It was considered therapeutic, and Lissa had discovered then that she enjoyed cooking.

'I'll get in touch with the agencies after the weekend,' she told Joel, glancing at her watch. 'It's time for the girls' tea. I'll go down and make it.'

She was surprised by the glimmer of amusement she saw in his eyes and blurted out defensively, 'What's wrong . . . why are you laughing?'

'It's hardly a traditional start to married life is it?' Joel murmured, one arched eyebrow inviting her to share his wry amusement. Lissa refused to respond. He alarmed her when he was relaxed and friendly with her; she found herself having to fight not to respond to him; she preferred it when he was coolly contemptuous and distant. Her fingers curled into her palms as she remembered that she was now his wife . . . that tonight . . . She went hot and cold as she remembered the savage fury with which she had accepted his proposal; the reprisals she had planned to punish him for the anguish he had caused her. Now she could hardly believe her own folly. How on earth had she expected to get away with it? Joel wasn't the man to allow her to change the rules of their relationship simply to suit herself. He expected her to be his wife in every sense of the word; to share his bed, and when he discovered that she could not . . . She shivered suddenly, freezing when he reached out and touched her arm. 'Cold?' He was frowning slightly as though the fact that she might be concerned him. Dear Heaven what would he *say* if she told him the truth? If she told him that she was as cold inside as perma-frost and that neither he nor any other man could melt it? How clearly she could recall her anguish when she first discovered her inability to respond sexually to anyone. She had been almost twenty before she had had another boyfriend—a quiet pleasant boy she had met at work, but the very first time he had kissed her she had been frozen by the mental image of Joel his touch conjured up. Shaking her head in an effort to dispel the past, Lissa managed a brief smile. 'No, not really. I'll take the girls downstairs and feed them. What do you want to do? Shall I make something for us later . . .

'What do you have in mind? A romantic candle-lit dinner *à deux*?' His eyes and voice held amusement, but it was a gentle amusement rather than a mocking one, and the rueful curl of his mouth showed that he wanted to share it with her. Against her will Lissa felt herself responding, a wry smile tugging at the corners of her own mouth.

'By the time I've fed and bathed these two, I'll probably be so tired all I'll want to do is fall straight into bed.'

She had spoken without thinking, lulled by the gentleness of his voice and eyes, and now hot colour flamed over her skin. Much to her chagrin her embarrassment only seemed to increase Joel's good humour.

'No . . . don't try to hide it,' he told her softly, when she tried to duck away. His fingers cupped her face. 'You know, when you blush like that I find it very hard to believe that you're the experienced woman you are. Mind you . . .' his voice dropped to a tormentingly sensual drawl, 'I find it extremely flattering that you're so anxious to . . . consummate our marriage.'

She hadn't meant that at all Lissa thought frantically, and he knew it. The fact that he could be so coolly amused over what had already caused her a sleepless night stung her into saying curtly, 'Well I shouldn't be if I were you . . . after all you know my reputation.'

For a moment he looked almost bitter, and then his expression changed, his voice smooth as he half purred with dangerous silkiness. 'Yes indeed and I shall look forward to discovering if you merit it.'

Lissa turned away, calling to the children. Why, oh why did he always manage to outflank her? She was regretting her impetuosity in agreeing to this marriage more and more with every second that passed, and yet when she looked into the happy faces of her nieces she couldn't entirely regret it. Already she felt a fierce upthrust of protective love for them, much stronger now than it had been when her sister was alive. How could she have allowed Joel to take them completely out of her life? The answer was that she could not, but neither should she have deceived him. When he proposed to her she should have told him the truth; that their marriage would have to be a platonic one.

All the time she was feeding and then preparing the girls for bed Lissa was conscious of nervous butterflies swarming in her stomach. She couldn't bear that . . . She couldn't bear to be parted from the children. At that moment he raised his head and looked across at her. 'You look tired.' The compassion in his face stirred her senses. For one wild, mad moment she almost allowed herself to believe that he genuinely cared about her welfare, and then she subdued the weakness. She had always viewed Joel with a certain amount of awe and dread, but she was coming to recognise that she had under-estimated his masculine power. She had thought him hard and aggressive and had prepared herself to withstand such macho maleness, but what she had not expected was this streak of tender concern; this warmth and caring that completely contradicted the mental image she had always had of him.

'Just a little.' She went across to the girls to kiss them good night, promising to leave the little night-light on.

'I'm glad you and Joel are going to be our new

mummy and daddy,' Louise said drowsily, kissing her back. 'But you won't ever leave us will you?' Anxiety clouded the blue eyes and Lissa hugged her fiercely. 'No, poppet, I promise I'll never leave you,' she whispered back. Poor little mite; how frightened and insecure she must feel at times. It would be her responsibility and her mission in life to give her back a sense of security and belonging.

'Dinner . . .' Joel said firmly, taking her arm and shepherding her out of the room.

Lissa almost sagged at the thought of having to go downstairs and prepare a meal. The ordeal of the ceremony had taken more out of her than she had realised.

'What would you like,' she asked Joel. 'I'll have a root round in the kitchen.'

'No need,' he surprised her by saying. 'It's all done. All you have to do is go and get changed.'

When he saw her surprise, he grinned, a surprisingly boyish grin that made him look years younger than his thirty-odd and for some reason Lissa felt her heart start to trip in tiny hammer blows that made it difficult for her to breathe. 'Don't look like that. All I've done is take something out of the freezer and put it in the oven. I did it whilst you were feeding the kids. I thought about taking you out to eat, but you look all in.' He glanced at his watch and announced, 'You've got half an hour.'

It took her twenty minutes to shower and change. Joel had been up to London and cleared her flat, and now all her clothes were hanging up in her new wardrobe. Her heart started to thud despairingly as she picked out a soft lilac Jean Muir dress she had bought on impulse. The colour brought out the rich red of her hair and the silky jersey clung lovingly to the sleek lines of her body, but Lissa was barely aware of how she looked, she was too concerned with what lay ahead. Would Joel expect her to move her things into his room or . . . If only she could just get through tonight . . . Dare she risk telling him that she could not be his wife? She bit her lip thinking of the promise she had just made to Louise.

'Play it by ear,' an inner voice told her. Joel wasn't a boyfriend after all . . . he might not even care whether she responded to him sexually or not . . . he might not even realise that . . . that she was a virgin and frigid as well? Don't be a fool, she cautioned herself. The man she had always imagined Joel to be might not have cared what she was and might indeed have simply been content to take his own pleasure without giving a thought to her, but the complex, sometimes sensitive man Joel was revealing himself to actually be would hardly be oblivious to the fact that she was not the experienced, almost promiscuous woman he thought her.

Frowning slightly Lissa brushed her hair. Why did Joel want their marriage to be consummated? Knowing the opinion he had of her he could hardly desire her that much, he had certainly never been short of female companionship . . . The answer lay in his love for Louise and Emma, Lissa decided. Like her he cared very deeply about his two nieces, and like her he obviously did not want a long drawn out legal battle over them.

But that did not answer her question, Lissa reflected thoughtfully. It showed why he might want to marry her; but not why he should want that marriage consummated. Unless prehaps he wanted a son . . . For some reason that thought made her heart beat faster, her mind's eye all too easily conjuring up the image of a small dark-haired baby with Joel's golden eyes.

Perhaps if she simply said nothing and let him discover . . . Shivering she pushed the problem out of her mind, coating her mouth with a soft lip gloss and then getting up. The more she dwelt on what lay ahead the more tense she got. If she carried on like this Joel was bound to realise something was wrong. What if he became furious and insisted on having their marriage annulled? Could she bear to lose the girls now?

'Lissa?'

The sound of his voice outside her door made her jump up from the dressing table and hurry across the room. 'Coming,' she called out, huskily, opening the door, coming to a full stop as she realised that Joel too had changed. Her eyes widened a little over the formality of his crisp white shirt and dinner suit, and then colour flooded her pale skin as she realised that he was studying her, his glance lingering appreciatively on the curves the lilac jersey seductively revealed.

'Why the embarrassment?' he asked, touching her cheek lightly with his finger. 'Surely by now you must be used to men finding you attractive.'

'I . . . I never think of myself that way.' She had made the admission before she was aware of it, adding more to herself than to him, 'I was always so gawky and plain as a teenager, especially compared with Amanda and my mother . . .'

'. . . that in an effort to prove to yourself and them that you were attractive you flung yourself into bed with every available male that came along?' Joel finished for her, but there was no accusation in his voice, no contempt either, Lissa noticed. In fact, if anything, the only emotion she could hear was a certain wry sadness. She risked a quick glance at Joel and found that he was smiling at her.

'I . . . I always felt that my parents preferred Amanda to me,' Lissa heard herself admitting huskily, much to her own astonishment.

'Yes, I know what you mean,' Joel agreed. 'John was always very much my father's favourite and there was a time when I over-reacted against that favouritism in an effort to draw my father's attention to myself.'

They had reached the top of the stairs and Lissa felt a wave of fellow-feeling towards him engulf her. She turned towards him but he forestalled her questions by saying quietly, 'We must make sure that neither Louise, nor Emma . . . nor indeed any children of our own we have, suffer that same burden.'

Instantly the rapport between them snapped as Lissa contained a shiver of fear and drew back slightly from him, her eyes unconsciously darkening. 'Who are you thinking about Lissa,' Joel grated. 'Simon Greaves? Then forget him,' he snapped. 'You're married to me not him.'

The abrupt change from compassionate fellow human being to arrogant male unnerved her, and she hurried down the stairs, turning towards the kitchen.

Warm, enticing aromas greeted her, but the wooden kitchen table was bare of all utensils. As she turned automatically to open drawers and collect cutlery Joel stopped her. 'It's all done,' he told her coolly, adding, 'I thought we'd dine in style tonight—in the dining room. You go through and sit down, and I'll bring the food.'

It was a novel experience for Lissa to be waited on by a man, but Joel did a superb job so calmly and efficiently that she must have betrayed her surprise, because he paused to smile at her and explained, 'I was in the army for a couple of years after leaving Oxford and if it taught me nothing else, it taught me to be self-sufficient.'

Lissa was surprised. She'd always thought that Joel had gone straight from university into his father's firm, and it was disturbing to realise how little she knew about him; and how guilty she was of having preconceived ideas about the type of man he was.

'Like you, as a teenager I was rebellious,' he further explained whilst they were eating. 'I wanted to travel . . . to see a little of the world before I settled down to the life my father wanted me to lead. I've always been more interested in the land than in industry, but as I was the eldest my father expected me to take over from him in the business. Later of course the situation resolved itself, but at twenty-two I couldn't see that far ahead and so I opted out—joined the army more in defiance of my father than anything else, but it's something I've never regretted. It . . .'

'Made a man of you?' quipped Lissa lightly, wanting to change the intimacy of their conversation, alarmed by the sensations and emotions he was arousing inside her. She didn't want to feel sympathy for him . . . she didn't want to feel anything. She wanted to hang on to her resentment and dislike. For some reason she needed to hang on to them. Why? she asked herself and knew the answer was because she felt it would be dangerous for her to get to know and like this man who was now her husband. Further than that she was not prepared to go.

'Not in the sense that I suspect you mean.' Joel's mouth twisted slightly and Lissa knew she had been successful in destroying his relaxed mood. 'More wine? You've barely touched yours. Don't you like it?'

The plain truth was that she was too tensed up to enjoy her meal at all, but dutifully she sipped the rich, ruby liquid, feeling it warm first her throat and then her stomach, relaxing over-taut nerves.

It was gone nine before they had finished their leisurely meal—or at least Joel had finished, she had done little more than toy with hers.

'Coffee?'

She shook her head tensely. 'No . . . no thanks. I'll take these things out to the kitchen.'

'I'll give you a hand.'

There was something disturbingly intimate about being in the kitchen with Joel, his easy, competent movements somehow pinpointing the uneasy tension of hers. When every last cup and plate had been cleared away he said easily, 'Why don't you go and check on the girls while I'm locking up? Oh and Lissa,' he added, less casually as he opened the door for her. 'Remember it's my room you're sleeping in tonight.'

Now was her time to tell him the truth, but Lissa knew that she couldn't. Trailing reluctantly upstairs she tried to convince herself that he might not notice her coldness; that it might not be as bad as she envisaged; that thousands upon thousands of women before her had endured the unwanted possession of the male sex. But Joel thought she was experienced and even worse eager for sex. Well he would soon learn the truth. All the fierce triumph she had felt at the thought of him being confronted with her innocence had gone, and a wild trembling seemed to seize hold of her limbs. She checked automatically on the two sleeping girls, leaving on the night-light in case one of them woke. The nursery was still relatively unfamiliar to them, and although on the surface they seemed to be accepting their parents' death, who knew what terrors their subconscious minds might harbour.

Knowing she could delay no longer Lissa turned in the direction of her own room, quickly gathering up her nightdress and robe. She daredn't linger here, because she wouldn't put it past Joel to come looking for her, and that was a humiliation she could not endure. She did not want to add cowardice to all her other faults.

Joel was already in the room, and he paused in the action of removing his shirt to look at her. The glow from a lamp illuminated the warm bronze of his skin. His chest was shadowed with a line of dark hair and Lissa felt her stomach plunge and twist crazily as though she were riding a switchback ride. No doubt most women would think she was crazy to fear Joel's possession so much. He was after all an extremely attractive man, and not just physically, she was forced to admit. He had a tender, gentle side to him that suggested that he would be a skilled and caring lover . . . A shudder washed over her, and watching it Joel frowned.

Lissa opened her mouth to tell him that there was no way she could go through with making love with him, but he anticipated her, shrugging off his shirt and coming across the room to take her hands in his. This close she could feel the heat coming off his body, smell the male scent of him, and she quivered nervously, her eyes huge and dark.

'Nervous? Me too,' he said softly.

Her surprise showed in her eyes and he added raspingly, 'Lissa, I *am* human too you know. I know quite well that you've married me for the sake of the girls and that reason alone; that right now I am not the man you want in your bed, but we could have a good life together . . . children of our own . . .'

'But . . . but what about love,' Lissa heard herself croak in an unsteady voice.

His hands dropped away from hers and he turned away from her. 'Can you honestly tell me that you've loved every man you've taken to your bed?' And as she heard the iron bitterness in his voice Lissa knew that her chance to tell him the truth was gone.

Looking at the situation from Joel's point of view it would seem all too logical that their relationship was a physical as well as legal one no doubt.

'Hell,' he swore briefly, 'I've forgotten something. Back in a minute.'

While he was gone Lissa dived into the bathroom, cleansing her face quickly and rushing into her nightdress. When she opened the bathroom door he still hadn't returned, and she scrambled into the huge double bed, firmly pulling the bedclothes up around her, tensing as the door opened.

Under his arm Joel was carrying an ice bucket and a bottle of champagne, two glasses in his hand. He raised his eyebrows queryingly as he put it down and a tiny ache began somewhere deep inside her. How would she be feeling right now, if things were different . . . if she loved Joel and he loved her . . . She could not deny his thoughtfulness and caring, and she could also sense the effort he was making to give their marriage some semblance of normality. Now she dreaded him knowing the truth for a different reason. She felt as though she were the one cheating him. But he had not married her for herself, she knew that. He had married her because she was the girls' aunt.

She heard the champagne cork pop and watched nervously as he filled the glasses. She had to sit up to take hers, and she could feel his eyes on her as she clutched the sheet to her body. The bubbles tickled her nose, making her catch her breath.

'Here's to us, Mrs Hargreaves,' Joel toasted softly. 'Shall we forget the past, Lissa, and have a new beginning?'

If only she could! If only she were really Joel's chosen bride, confident of his love . . . The thought jolted through her making her tremble. What was she *thinking*? It must be the champagne, she thought dizzily. She didn't want Joel to love her. Why should she?

He disappeared into the bathroom, and she listened to him moving about, every muscle tense, her body aching with dread. Memories from the past threatened to swamp over her, and when Joel finally emerged from the bathroom, she could only stare at him with unseeing eyes. He was wearing a towelling robe, his legs bare beneath the hem, she noticed, her glance skittering away and yet somehow drawn back to his body. She was twenty-three for God's sake, she derided herself mentally, not fifteen. But deep inside herself she was still only fifteen, locked for ever in the torment of a nightmare that featured this dark-haired man, who was now shedding his robe and getting into bed beside her.

'Lissa?' He tensed suddenly and for a moment Lissa thought he must have guessed the truth, but then he was frowning, throwing the bedclothes aside and pulling on his robe.

'I can hear one of the girls crying,' he told her tautly. 'Listen.'

CHAPTER FIVE

If anyone had ever told her that she would spend her wedding night comforting a distraught four year old she would never have believed them Lissa thought tiredly, glancing at her watch. Four o'clock in the morning and they had finally got Louise off to sleep.

'You go back to bed,' Joel told her. 'I'll sit with her now.'

It had taken both of them to calm the little girl out of her nightmare fears, but she had clung fiercely to them both once she was awake, refusing to let them go, only when Lissa had promised to stay with her, had she finally allowed Joel to go downstairs and make her a drink. Now she was sleeping at last, like Emma who had fortunately remained fast asleep throughout the whole thing.

As she crawled back into Joel's bed, Lissa reflected with niggling impatience that she ought to be feeling relieved that Louise's timely nightmare had occurred, but instead what she did feel was something almost approaching a sense of anti-climax. Surely she couldn't have *wanted* Joel to make love to her? Of course not . . . Then why this strange restless sensation that was gripping her, when in reality all she ought to be doing was dropping into an exhausted sleep?

Joel woke her at seven o'clock. A dark shadow covered his jaw and his hair was ruffled untidily.

'Sorry to wake you,' he apologised, 'but I've got to be at the factory at nine—a meeting that was arranged some time ago. I'll have a shower and get changed . . . If you could keep an eye on Louise, although I think she'll be okay now.'

'Has she had many nightmares like that?' Lissa asked him. He looked tired and drawn and she had a crazy impulse to touch him, to smooth the lines of tiredness away from his eyes.

'None quite as bad as that.' He turned towards the bathroom and Lissa slithered out of bed, tensing as he turned round unexpectedly and came over to her. Her nightdress was a long one and demure, but the bright February sunshine made the fine cotton almost transparent and the way Joel was looking at her made it impossible for her to move, even when he reached out and gently pulled her towards him.

'Good morning Mrs Hargreaves,' he murmured against her ear, his breath tickling her skin, sending tiny shimmers of sensation coursing over it. 'That was some wedding night wasn't it?'

She turned her head opening her mouth to respond, her words silenced by the warm pressure of Joel's lips caressing her own. Shivers of something that was not entirely fear raced through her. She made an inarticulate protest, surprised to find that Joel was holding her quite tightly, drawing her against his body, so that she was aware of the heavy thump of his heart and the warmth of his skin, and then she pulled away relieved when Joel released her.

'Perhaps you're right,' he muttered smiling at her. 'There isn't time now for me to make love to you as I want to. Surprised that I should desire you, Lissa?' he asked apparently reading her mind with ease.

'I thought you didn't like me ... that you disapproved of me ...' She made the admission slowly, still a little stunned to find that her mind clung obstinately to the memory of how his mouth had felt against hers.

He studied her quietly for a moment and then said slowly, 'Perhaps neither of us entered this marriage for the most altruistic of reasons, Lissa, but we *are* married, and I vote that as from now we put the past behind us, and make a completely fresh start.'

When seconds ticked by without her making any response, he released her almost abruptly, his eyes darkening, and his expression losing the elusive tenderness she had thought she glimpsed in it, and reverting to that she was more used to seeing— hard and unyielding, but Lissa was too stunned by her own thoughts and emotions to pay more than fleeting attention to Joel's tightlipped anger. Her heart was still thudding heavily with the shock of discovering how close she had come to agreeing with Joel's suggestion. Put the past behind them! She suppressed a half hysterical sound of pain in her throat. If only she could! But Joel didn't know what her past really was; and it was folly almost to the point of madness to allow herself to even think of responding to the half whimsical, half tender entreaty his words had seemed to hold. She must be going crazy, she thought over an hour later, still unable to banish Joel's image and his words from her brain. He made her feel vulnerable in a way that no other male had ever been able to do, and whilst Lissa acknowledged that much of this vulnerability sprang from the past; at least some of it was new. Shivering slightly she paced the kitchen floor. What was happening to her? Why after all these years of hating and resenting Joel was she now seeing another side to him; a side she had never imagined existed? Why . . . last night she had almost envied Louise because of his tenderness towards the little girl. She curled her fingers into the palms of her hands, swinging round abruptly and going upstairs. Emma was awake, but Louise was still asleep, worn out by the trauma of her nightmares.

Since they were now without a housekeeper she would at least have plenty to occupy her hands if not her mind, Lissa reflected grimly when she had washed and dressed Emma.

But keeping her hands busy did nothing to still the restless tension of her thoughts. She had been a fool to marry Joel . . . she couldn't have a normal marriage with him. Even at the thought of it odd tremors raced over suddenly hot flesh, her body trembling as though he were already touching it, caressing her . . . Emma gazed round-eyed at her as she suddenly clapped her hands over her ears and groaned out loud. What was happening to her? Why was she feeling like this? Why now after all these years was she suddenly experiencing this conflict within herself?

By lunchtime Louise was awake, and Lissa had just settled both girls down to a light meal, when the 'phone rang.

The sound of Joel's voice on the other end of the line made the tiny hairs on her arm stand on end, his curt, 'Lissa, is something wrong?' making her glad that he could not see her pale face and betraying eyes.

'I'm just a bit tired that's all,' she told him coolly.

He asked about the girls and then told her that he had to go up to London on business and would not be back until the morning.

Having assured him that Louise seemed quite recovered, Lissa let him ring off. There was no reason in the world why she should feel this sharp stab of something very close to disappointment, no reason at all and yet she did. It came to her then, as she walked back to the girls that she had always enjoyed their encounters in the past and that she had actually derived a certain savage pleasure in her confrontations with Joel. Shaking her head over the complexity of her own emotions she tried to dismiss him from her thoughts.

By the time she had got the girls bathed and in bed, Lissa felt extremely tried. She had telephoned the local paper during the afternoon to place an 'ad' for a cook-cum-housekeeper, and she had also spent some time exploring the house.

Although much of the decor was not to her taste, the house itself appealed strongly to her, and as she wandered from room to room she found herself mentally refurbishing them, making plans for a future here she was not sure she had. What would Joel do if she told him the truth?

If? Lissa grimaced inwardly. There was no if about it. She had to. She had come to that decision during the afternoon. Now that the fierce hunger for revenge which had eaten away at her had gone, she knew she had little alternative. Joel was not the monster she had always told herself he was. She had only to see him with the children to know that, and Lissa knew that much of the resentment and bitterness she had hoarded against him had had its roots in her feelings towards her father—*he* was the one who had rejected her, but because at fifteen she had been unable to cope with such ambivalent feelings towards her parents as love and resentment, she had focused her resentment on Joel. She sighed faintly. She was not telling herself anything she did not already know. Several years ago she had made herself re-live the traumatic years of her teens and had taught herself then to analyse what she had experienced, but she had never totally thrown off her hatred of Joel . . . Until now.

Too emotionally restless to settle she wandered tensely from room to room, pausing occasionally to study a portrait or an object without really seeing them. It was one thing to know and accept that much of her resentment of Joel was something she had transferred from her father's shoulders to his, but that did not explain away the sexual trauma she experienced whenever she was with someone else. Why should it always be Joel's image that rose up to taunt her when another man held her in his arms; why not her father's angry, forbidding features?

And why the overwhelming complex tangle of emotions she experienced whenever he was close to her? Both were questions she could not answer, any more than she could turn back time and control the tide of anger which had swept her into this marriage in the first place.

At last she settled in the sitting room, switching on the television but watching it without taking anything in. It was too early to go to bed yet—she would never sleep, and the evening stretched emptily ahead of her. The house felt different without Joel in it. What was the matter with her she chastised herself. Good heavens how many evenings had she spent alone in her London flat without feeling the slightest desire for anyone else's company?

She curled up in one of the easy chairs, tucking her feet underneath her, gradually letting the tension ease out of her body. As soon as an opportunity presented itself to her, she must tell Joel the truth. If she didn't and he went through with his intention of making her his wife physically as well as legally he would discover some of it at least for himself anyway, and the childish desire for revenge which had carried her into their marriage now seemed childish and incredibly foolish. What good would it really serve either of them for him to discover the hard way that physically she was unable to respond to him, other than to prove how wrong his judgments of her were? The satisfaction she would gain would be nothing when set against her embarrassment and mortification. It had been very hard for her to accept that some vital element of her femininity had been destroyed, and she couldn't bear to lie and watch the vagrant tenderness she had thought she glimpsed in his eyes this morning, turning to bitter contempt. She had experienced the angry and frustrated reactions of too many men already for her to be in any doubt about Joel's.

And worse he would guess that she had deliberately withheld the truth from him and why. She had seen a different side of him these last few days; one she had never guessed he possessed, and it caused a strange yearning emotion inside her.

Her eyes closed and she let her thoughts drift, ranging backwards in time and then forwards, gradually relaxing into sleep.

'Lissa?'

She woke with a start, looking uncertainly towards the door which Joel had just opened.

The unexpectedness of seeing him there disorientated her. She glanced at her watch, surprised to realise how long she had been asleep. It was gone twelve o'clock.

'Joel!' she exclaimed in a sleepy, surprised voice. 'What are you doing back?'

She tried to move as she spoke, gasping in pain as pins and needles attacked her legs. Her own fault for falling asleep with them tucked up like that.

'Perhaps I couldn't bear to stay away.'

Joel's hands on her wrists, firmly folding her hands in her lap before they moved to her legs, shocked her into immobility. He spoke calmly enough, his voice so devoid of inflection that it was impossible for her to interpret whatever motive lay behind what he was saying. Was he being sarcastic, or simply making a light joke? She shivered, as his fingers touched her skin, rubbing the tingling sensation away.

'Are you all right?'

Now she could hear something in his voice, concern and something else she couldn't name, that made it rough and slightly husky. She could tell that he was frowning without looking up at him, and guessed that he was aware of her tension; of the way she tried to escape his touch.

'Fine,' she lied, giving him a brittle, tight smile. 'I think I'll go up . . .' She squirmed away from him, hoping he would move, but he kept his hands either side of her on the chair arms.

'Something *is* wrong. What is it, Lissa?' He turned away from her abruptly, but she was too tense to get up. 'It's too late now for second thoughts; for wishing that I was Greaves.'

'I don't . . .' The denial was blurted out before she could retract it, and she felt a curious twist of emotion curl through her heart as he frowned down at her; a combination of fear and an excitement she could not analyse; a tiny thrill of apprehension.

'No? But you did shrink away from me,' he told her softly. 'Why, Lissa? Oh I know there's always been a degree of antagonism between us, but you're not naïve, you know as well as I do that it's an antagonism sparked by mutual desire.' He looked grimly at her, and continued before she could speak. 'Neither of us might be proud of desiring the other, but I know if we're honest that neither of us could deny it.'

He caught the small sound she choked back and stared at her, watching the colour drain out of her face.

'Lissa, for God's sake.' He sounded more angry than concerned and Lissa flinched back from him as he added, 'Let's stop the play-acting shall we? A physical relationship between us was part and parcel of the deal when you agreed to marry me. You knew that . . .'

'Are you trying to tell me you married me solely because you wanted to go to bed with me?' Lissa was proud of the cool way she threw the taunt at him.

'Don't be ridiculous. You know damn well I

didn't. After all why the hell should I go to such lengths to secure something other men—plenty of other men have had for ...' He caught her hand just before it connected with his jaw, gripping her wrist so tightly that it hurt. 'Cut out the injured innocent bit, Lissa ... it doesn't suit you.'

She was practically trembling with rage and yes with pain too, hating him for what he was saying to her; for revealing to her how he really viewed her. It was intolerable, unbearable ... and to think she had contemplated telling him the truth! She could not endure to stay here a moment longer ... The girls ... all the logical calm thinking she had done during the day were forgotten ... Nothing was more important than escaping from Joel and the agony he was causing her.

'Let me go.' She rubbed her aching wrists, as he released her, scrambling off the chair and moving on shaking legs towards the door.

'Lissa ...'

'Don't touch me!' Her throat was so tight with pain she could barely speak, her voice a husky whisper of torment. 'Don't come anywhere near me! I'm leaving, now ... this minute. I ...' To her bitter humiliation tears clogged her throat, filling her eyes, and threatening to flood humiliatingly from her eyes. She felt so weak and alone ... desperate for some haven in which to hide away from him, and yet knowing she had none.

'Lissa!' He ignored her demands, striding towards her, catching hold of her arm with strong fingers. Panic exploded through her in wave after wave of sheer terror. She was back at the party, fifteen again, only this time Joel wasn't just looking at her, he was touching her, hurting her physically as well as mentally. She gave a thin, high scream of pain, grateful for the deep heavy black void that opened up to receive her and grant her oblivion.

Lissa opened her eyes reluctantly and stared round the shadowed bedroom. Where was she? Suddenly she remembered and she shuddered. This was Joel's room. No *their* room, she corrected herself, bitterly. He must have brought her here after . . . after she'd fainted. She must get away . . . She must escape before he hurt her any more. She sat up groggily, swinging her feet to the floor.

'Lissa!'

The peremptory command in his voice as Joel walked into the room froze her. He was carrying a tray with a cup of tea on it.

'Drink this.' He put the cup down on the bedside table nearest to her, 'And then you and I are going to talk.' He looked so grimly angry that Lissa started to tremble; her teeth chattering together as wave after wave of fear shuddered through her. She heard Joel swear and saw him come towards her, holding out her hands to ward him off. And then suddenly and unnervingly she was crying . . . deep, wrenching sobs that hurt her chest and made her whole body shake.

'Shush .. shush ... it's all right ...' Unbelievably being rocked in Joel's arms, with the warm pressure of his body against her own, created inside her an intense sensation of security and comfort. She wanted to cling to him Lissa realised numbly, to burrow against him and let the soft words he was murmuring soothe and relax her. But it was *Joel* who had provoked the emotional storm now racking her; Joel with his cruel jibing tongue who was responsible for her pain. It was also Joel who was easing it, she acknowledged hazily, Joel was making her feel cherished and cared for.

By the time the tearing sobs were under control she had recovered enough to want to pull away from him, deeply embarrassed and confused by her own behaviour, but Joel wouldn't let her, subsiding on to the side of the bed, and taking her with him, still holding her in his arms.

'Now,' he said quietly, 'I want to know what all that was about.'

Lissa managed a tight smile. 'Oh just another trick in my repertoire,' she told him brittley. 'Very effective isn't it?'

For a long moment he simply looked at her, and then he said quietly, 'Extremely effective; so much so that I find it impossible to believe it was fabricated. And so no doubt you are going to tell me, was your faint.' He watched the colour run up under her skin and said sardonically, 'Exactly.

'I've seen fear before, Lissa, and I've seen panic, and I know when they're genuine. What I don't know is why *I* should invoke them so forcefully in you.'

Now there was no going back. She would have to tell him, Lissa knew, and coupled with apprehension and reluctance was also relief. She wanted to tell him; she wanted to be rid of the emotional burden she was carrying.

Lifting her head she answered simply, 'Because you want us to be lovers,' and was rewarded by a physical reaction every bit as violent in its own way as her own had been. Dark colour burned up under his skin, stretching it somehow until it was pulled sharply over his cheek bones. His eyes glittered darkly with a mixture of anger and something else she couldn't put a name to, his fingers curling round her wrist as he said grimly, 'You have a hell of a way of putting a man down, Lissa. I won't ask what it is that bars me from joining the ranks of those fortunate enough to enjoy your favours—I dare not . . .'

'No . . . no . . . you don't understand,' Lissa interrupted impetuously, determined now that she had committed herself to honesty to go through with it. 'It isn't you . . . at least, it is, but . . . Oh look, Joel, let me go right back to the beginning.'

He released her wrist, and watched grimly as she moved back from him, putting a distance between them.

'I can't let you be my lover . . . or indeed any man be my lover because . . . because I . . . find the thought of sex . . . What I'm trying to tell you is that I'm . . . I'm frigid,' she said flatly at last. 'I've never had sex with anyone, Joel,' she told him forcing herself to look at him and forestalling what she knew he must be going to say by saying quickly, 'Yes, I know you must find that hard to believe but it's true. That night, that party, when I was fifteen . . . that was the first time . . .' She swallowed, trying to concentrate on a piece of wallpaper safely taking her eyes away from Joel's and allowing her to continue her story without having to look at him and see how he was reacting.

'Nothing really happened . . . just a little very light petting . . .'

'Your father told me you were wildly promiscuous,' Joel broke in curtly. 'Are you trying to tell me . . .'

'My father and I didn't get on . . . I was extremely rebellious . . . but never in that way. My parents disapproved of my crowd of friends. I'd been forbidden to go out that night . . . but I disobeyed them—for the first and last time,' she added wryly. 'My father was an extremely strict man. Amanda knew how to get round him, but I didn't have the knack. You see,' she said with painful honesty, 'I was never what he wanted in a daughter, I wasn't blonde and small and cuddly like my mother and Amanda and . . . Oh well no doubt much of it was my fault, because I never tried to conform to what he wanted me to do . . . You see I wanted him . . . both of them to love me for what I was . . . not as another Amanda, but you know how teenagers are, I couldn't articulate any of this to them. My father disapproved of teenagers anyway . . . Every time he read about teenage misdemeanours in the press he used to go on about it . . . I wasn't promiscuous at all . . . I suspect he confused you with what he no doubt described as my appalling behaviour; he did rather have a tendency for exaggeration. Of course the fact that I'd disobeyed him and then been found by him in the circumstances that I was . . . It was all quite innocent really, but he would never believe that . . .'

'I had no idea.' Joel was frowning now. 'He'd described you to my parents as extremely rebellious and wild. When he asked me to come with him and fetch you back from that party, I naturally assumed . . .'

'The worst!' Lissa supplied briefly. 'Yes . . . I can understand that.'

'So, given, that at fifteen you were innocent of the crimes attributed to you, I don't see . . .' He frowned and then said slowly, 'Lissa, are you trying to tell me that you're still a virgin?'

'I'm afraid so . . . Oh not by choice,' she assured him grimly. 'Being virginal at fifteen is one thing, being in the same state at twenty-three is quite definitely another, but . . .' She got up off the bed, and paced the floor tensely, now that she was faced with telling him, at a loss to know how to.

'But *what*, Lissa?' It was plain that Joel was completely bemused, 'And don't try telling me that it is through lack of opportunity.'

'No not that,' Lissa agreed drily, 'but because of what happened at that party I seem to have developed a mental block where sex is concerned. No matter how much I might think I want to make love when it comes to it I can't, because all I see is . . .'

'Your father's angry, disapproving face,' Joel guessed tersely, his mouth compressing grimly. 'Yes, I can understand that.'

Just for one cowardly moment Lissa was tempted to agree and let matters go at that. Her heart was thumping crazily with a mixture of adrenalin and reaction. She wanted to take the way out Joel was unknowingly offering her, but something, some stubborn quirk of pride would not let her, and so instead she shook her head.

'No?' Joel frowned. 'Then what? Tell me, Lissa? What?' he demanded getting up and taking hold of her. 'What?' he repeated, watching as she touched her tongue to dry, stiff lips.

'You,' she choked out at last, refusing to look at him, her body tensing against his grip as she pulled instinctively away, fearing his reaction, dreading that if she did look at him she would see in his eyes the contempt that had haunted her dreams for so long. 'I see you,' she repeated instead in a low, tormented voice, 'and you look at me with such contempt and dislike that I . . .' She started to shake again, dimly aware of Joel cursing as he released her.

'Me? Lissa, look at me!' His hands gripping her face forced her to do as he wished. He was nearly as pale as she was herself but this was a different pallor, and Lissa shrank beneath the raw fury she could see glittering in his eyes until he said tersely, 'No, Lissa . . . Don't be frightened.'

'I shouldn't have told you.' She was mortified now by what she had revealed to him, unable to fully comprehend the reasons for the emotional outburst which she knew had been the release valve, allowing her to tell him the truth.

'But you have.' He looked at her in silence for several seconds, and then said abruptly, 'Is that why you agreed to marry me? As some sort of punishment . . . Or at least is that part of the reason?'

He was far too astute Lissa thought hollowly. 'Initially,' she agreed, in an expressionless voice. She felt far too drained to endure any more emotions. 'But only because you had made me so very angry. Once my anger had cooled I wanted to retract, but then there were the girls to consider . . . I thought it would pay you back, you see,' she said simply, 'but of course once my temper had gone I realised how stupid I was being . . . After all it wasn't even your fault that I . . .'

'No ... it wasn't *my* fault at all,' Joel agreed harshly. 'No ... *I* can't be blamed for condemning you out of hand, can I, Lissa? After all *I* wasn't fifteen was I? I was well into my twenties ... and naturally it is perfectly understandable that I should have destroyed the fragile illusions of someone little more than a child ... that I should have accepted someone else's valuation of you without forming my own. No, of course *I* can't be blamed. Like hell I can't,' he added bitterly, turning away from her. 'Like hell.'

For a moment there was silence, while Lissa struggled to come to terms with Joel's savage reaction to her disclosures. She had seen him exhibit tenderness and concern for his nieces; and she had known there was a gentler side to him, but she had never expected this devastating reaction to her revelations; this rage of anger directed against himself.

At last he said curtly, 'And so what now? Do you want the marriage annulled? It could be.'

Did she? With a sudden, stifling leap of her heart Lissa knew she did not without quite knowing why. All she could manage to say was a rather unsteady, 'Do you?'

'What does that mean?' Joel questioned. 'That you wish to stay married to me perhaps, but in name only, because of the girls?'

Gratefully Lissa seized on the opening he had given her. 'Yes ...' she agreed quickly. 'Yes ... I couldn't bear to lose them now. I feel that they need both of us, Joel, just as you said but of course, now that you know that ... that I ... that ...'

'That I can't make love to you,' he supplied harshly for her.

'Yes . . . yes,' Lissa agreed hurriedly. 'If because of that you want to be free . . .'

She found during the silence that followed that she was holding her breath, hoping that he would not say that he wanted to end their marriage she acknowledged inwardly.

'I owe you some recompense,' he said at last, 'and if marriage to me is what you want, Lissa . . . then that is what you shall have, but there is one thing I shall insist on.' He looked at her and then said coolly, 'We must continue to share this room. As much for the girls' sake as anything else. They've already been through far too much. You of all people will know how sensitive and quick children can be. They're used to their parents sleeping together and I believe that if we show any deviation from that pattern it could cause Louise more anxiety.'

Lissa nodded her head slowly. There was something in what Joel was saying, and what he asked was very little.

'What?' he queried when she assented. 'No demand for my solemn promise that I won't touch you?'

Lissa looked at him in surprise. 'But why should you want to?' she asked him, genuinely puzzled. 'You can hardly want me now. You're forgetting, Joel,' she reminded him wryly, 'I know *exactly* how off-putting men find my . . . my disability. I know you said you wanted me, but that was when you thought I was sexually experienced . . . able to respond to you . . .'

'Yes, so it was,' he agreed quietly, and just for a

second something intangible, a fleeting expression in his eyes made a frisson of sensation run down her spine. Before she could analyse it, it was gone, and then Joel was saying curtly, 'Lissa, tell me have you ever discussed any of this with anyone else . . .'

'No.' She looked at him in fresh surprise. 'Somehow I've never been able to.'

'I see.' He wasn't looking at her and Lissa was sure she must have imagined the tiny thread of satisfaction running through his voice because when he did look at her, his face was carefully devoid of all expression.

'It's been a long day,' he said quietly. 'I think we should both try to get some sleep.' He picked up the now cold cup of tea he had made her earlier and said calmly, 'I'll go down and make us both a nightcap while you get ready for bed,' and Lissa knew that he was telling her that he was giving her the privacy to get undressed and into bed without him being there. She was grateful to him for his understanding, she thought tiredly as she slid between cool sheets a little later, and yet as she closed her eyes and tried to court sleep, the memory uppermost in her mind was of the emotional and physical sensations she had experienced when Joel held her in his arms.

CHAPTER SIX

'BUT you haven't kissed Lissa "goodbye".'

They were having breakfast in the kitchen, the scene a homely familiar one, Emma struggling with her cereal in her high chair while Louise sat between Joel and herself. Joel had an early meeting with one of his tenant farmers and he had already finished his breakfast. He had stood up to kiss Louise 'goodbye'—a formality she insisted on every morning, and it was her shrill, piping complaint that drew Lissa's attention away from Emma. Both of them were on their guard for any signs of insecurity from Louise, and over the top of her blonde head their eyes met in mutual concern. Since the night she had admitted the truth to him Lissa had found herself much more relaxed in Joel's company; much more able to appreciate the side of him she had previously thought reserved only for others. He was a compassionate caring man, and a very strong one as well, she acknowledged. He had talked to her on several occasions about her past, drawing her out in a way that afterwards had the power to amaze her. She had found herself confiding things to him that she had never dreamed of telling anyone, but conversely the closer she felt drawn towards him the greater pains he seemed to take to preserve a distance between them. And somehow that hurt, even though it should not have done.

'Kiss Mummy,' Emma announced, spooning

cereal liberally into and around her mouth. While Louise alternated in calling them Lissa and Joel and 'Mummy' and 'Daddy', Emma, too young to have any deeply lasting memory of her parents, had quickly transferred their titles to Lissa and Joel.

Both of them had agreed to let the girls call them whatever made them feel most comfortable, but it did something to her heart, Lissa admitted wryly, to hear Emma addressing her as 'Mummy'. She loved both girls with a fiercely protective maternalism that still half surprised her. They had entirely different personalities; in Louise she detected certain of her own personality traits, together with, quite surprisingly, some of Joel's, while Emma was completely Amanda's daughter.

Conscious of Louise's critically appraising scrutiny, Lissa obediently lifted her face in the direction of Joel's as he bent towards her. His mouth touched her cheek, his lips cool and firm, and a tiny shiver ran through her. She started to pull away, but his hand curled round the back of her head, his thumb tilting her jaw. For one surprised second her eyes stared into his, noting that close to they weren't flat, metallic gold at all, but warm and alive, glittering with topaz depths and then his mouth was on hers and instinctively her eyelashes fluttered down, her heartbeat surging into a faster tempo. Her body melted into soft pliancy with a swiftness that startled her, her lips enjoying the tactile sensation of Joel's moving against them. His grip on the back of her neck suddenly tightened and for a moment Lissa thought that he was actually going to kiss her properly, but then he released her stepping back, his mouth twisting in a derisive smile that reminded her of the old Joel she had resented so much.

'Daddy gone,' Emma exclaimed mournfully as the kitchen door closed behind him, and Lissa automatically directed her to finish up her breakfast, at the same time unable to stop her fingers from touching her still tremulous mouth, startled by the realisation that she had actually wanted Joel to kiss her. Why . . . why should Joel be able to arouse inside her a physical response that she was unable to give to anyone else?

It was probably because he knew the truth, she told herself and that because of that she was able to relax with him . . . knowing that she had nothing to fear; neither his anger nor his rejection. And after all he was an extremely attractive specimen of the male species she reminded herself wryly. She had grown so used to seeing Joel in his role as caring and concerned father-figure-cum-confessor that she was beginning to lose sight of the fact that he was also an extremely virile, sensual male. The thought was a disquieting one. At the moment Joel felt guilty enough about the past, and concerned enough for her and the girls for them to absorb all his spare time, but what would happen in the future when they were not such immediate concerns? When the girls were secure enough not to need so much attention? He was not a man she could ever envisage living like a monk . . . So he would take a mistress, a tiny voice told her coolly. What else could she expect? How could she object? How indeed? But more important why should she want to object? She didn't want Joel as her lover . . . did she?

That she should entertain even the slightest doubt rocked her into hurried action . . . anything to dispel such dangerous thoughts. Quickly she cleared away the breakfast things and got the girls buttoned into warm clothes so that she could take them for a walk.

Winterly had extensive gardens and Lissa took the girls outside for a walk most mornings. It was still only February, and although the weather was relatively mild there was definitely a chilly nip in the air.

They were out for almost an hour, returning with rosy cheeks and bright eyes, Emma now in Lissa's arms.

She had just put her down when the 'phone started to ring. Lissa picked up the receiver, delighted when she realised the woman on the other end of the line was calling in response to her ad for a new housekeeper. She lived locally, her caller told Lissa, and had been widowed eighteen months ago. In her late fifties she found herself with time on her hands and although she had had no previous working experience, she sounded so warm and pleasant that Lissa made an appointment to interview her.

With someone else to take over the more mundane household duties she would have more time to spend with the girls and some to spare to help Joel with his paper work. He had had a secretary who had come in a couple of days a week he had explained to her, but she had left the area when she married, and now he was relying on John's secretary at the factory complex, which was really an unsatisfactory arrangement. 'Mrs Hartwell already has more than enough to do,' he had told Lissa when they were discussing the matter, 'and once the new Managing Director is appointed, it would hardly be fair of me to appropriate his secretary's time for estate work.'

'Once we've got a new housekeeper I could help out here,' Lissa had offered, and she remembered now the way he had looked at her, thoughtfully almost as though he were trying to see into her mind.

'You already do more than enough,' he had told her rather abruptly. 'Just because you're my wife, Lissa, I don't expect you to work yourself into the ground.'

'But can't you see, I want to do it,' she had retorted. 'I want to help you as much as I can Joel . . . I need to be able to justify to myself my role as your wife,' she had admitted, surprising herself by her honesty.

'Do you?' The expression in his eyes then had been one she couldn't interpret, but she had moved quickly away from him, alerted by some primitive instinct to do so, although quite what she had feared she had been at a loss to know. Certainly his mouth had curled into a distinctly cynical smile, and he had said in that quiet, silky, even voice of his which she had learned to recognise was one he used when he was particularly irritated, 'There's no need to run away, Lissa, I'm not going to pounce on you . . .'

Lissa had been immediately ashamed of her reaction. Not once in the three weeks since she had told him the truth had Joel given the slightest indication of wanting to touch her in any way. At first her relief in having told him the truth blotted out any other emotions but now . . .

Now what? she challenged herself as she made the girls' lunch. She was disappointed because Joel had kept to his word? Of course not. How ridiculous . . . How could she be?

She had arranged to see Mrs Fuller, the applicant for the housekeeper's post while the girls had their afternoon nap, and when she answered the door to her knock Lissa was agreeably pleased with what she saw.

Small and slightly plump, Mrs Fuller had an air of warmth about her that Lissa immediately liked. As she showed her over the house she explained the type of life they led, adding, 'Of course the girls will not be your concern, but they *are* part of the household and both Joel and myself want them to feel secure and happy here. I do believe in a certain amount of discipline, but if for instance you feel that you couldn't cope with muddy boots in the kitchen occasionally or toys in the hall then this post won't be for you,' Lissa said firmly, feeling relieved when Mrs Fuller laughed warmly.

'Heavens, no, I think children make a home. I had three myself. They're all married now and living away from the home. Both my girls live abroad—one in Australia the other in California, so unfortunately I don't get to see my grandchildren often enough, but I do know what it means to have young children about the place. Of course there'll be certain rooms that you won't want them to play in.'

'The drawing room, my husband's study and the formal dining room,' Lissa agreed.

They talked for a little while longer, and when Mrs Fuller eventually left having agreed to start work the following Monday Lissa was extremely pleased.

She told Joel about it over dinner, checking as she wondered if perhaps he would have preferred to interview Mrs Fuller himself.

'Good heavens no,' he told her when she asked. 'That is entirely your province and if you say she's the right person for the job then I'm sure she is.'

He went on to tell her about the interviews he had been conducting to find a Managing Director to take over the running of the factory.

'I've managed to narrow it down to three,' he told her. 'I'm doing the final interviews tomorrow. I'll be glad when it's all sorted out.'

He looked tired Lissa realised, her frown deepening when she realised as well that he had lost a little weight. He had removed his suit jacket before he sat down for dinner and the fine silk of his shirt moved fluidly against his skin as he shifted in his seat. A strange, unfamiliar tension gripped her, her mouth suddenly dry, a pulse beating through her body with heavy forcefulness.

'Lissa?'

She realised that she was staring at him and dragged her gaze away, wondering if perhaps she was coming down with something. She felt so odd.

'Lissa, are you okay?' He stretched across the table, his fingers circling her wrist, his touch wholly clinical but it was like having a manacle of fire on her wrist. In shocked stupor Lissa found that she was looking at his mouth; remembering the cool strength of it against her own that morning. Something approaching faintness seemed to creep over her. She pulled away from him and tried to stand up, her legs refusing to support her properly.

'Lissa?'

Joel got up too, concerned for her, his eyes, as they always did when he was worried darkening slightly. She knew so much about him now she thought hazily, shaking her head, and telling him that she was fine; little insignificant things she hadn't even known she knew until now . . . like the way the dark hairs grew against his skin . . . the way his eyes changed colour, betraying him despite the control he seemed to have over his features. She could even faithfully recall the way he moved, simply by closing her eyes and picturing him. She was familiar with the masculine contours of his torso—at least visually. He wore pyjama bottoms in bed—for her benefit, she was sure, and she hadn't realised until now how often she had silently studied the hard male lines of his body. Hot colour touched her skin, scorching it as her thoughts were scorching her mind.

'I'll go and make the coffee,' she said hurriedly.

They had fallen into the habit of continuing the conversation begun over the dinner table through coffee and often until quite late in the evening. Joel was interesting to listen to, and he made Lissa feel that he valued her opinions. She had never enjoyed anyone's company as much as she enjoyed his and it came to her as she busied herself in the kitchen that if he were to leave her life now, there would be an acutely painful void. But the fact that she found him good company and mentally stimulating did not account for her rapid pulse and accelerated breathing . . . neither did it account for the disturbing physical response she had just experienced. She wasn't totally naïve; she had felt physical desire before even if it had only been fleetingly. But this was different . . . this was Joel.

She couldn't desire Joel. Why not, an inner voice demanded to know? Why *shouldn't* she desire him? Because . . . because . . . Because what? The same voice jeered. Because you'd convinced yourself you hated him? Because you resented the fact that as a teenager he found you totally uninteresting until the night of that party.

Lissa bit down hard on her bottom lip, trying to quell her rebellious thoughts. It was true, she was forced to acknowledge with painful honesty, that on the very brief occasions on which she had seen Joel before that night—and they had been fleeting in the extreme—she had been instantly struck by the masculine aura he carried about him. Amanda had caught her staring at him once with rounded eyes and had teased her about it.

'For goodness sake don't go and develop a crush on Joel,' she had warned her. 'He eats little girls like you for breakfast.'

Unwilling to follow her thoughts any further, Lissa made the coffee and carried it through into the sitting room. Joel was reading a farming magazine which he put down to take the tray from her, asking briefly, 'Okay now?'

When Lissa nodded he added. 'I'm sorry I missed the girls' bedtime tonight. I'll be glad when I've got the responsibility for the factory off my hands. I've been neglecting my own work recently . . . and I don't intend to be just a figurehead in the girls' lives—someone they hear about but rarely see. As my own father was to me,' he added, surprising her with this information about his childhood.

'Oh yes,' he told her obviously reading her mind. 'Like you, I was very much second best as far as my father was concerned. He and I never hit it off the way he and John did, although my childhood was nothing like as traumatic as yours.'

'Mine was bad because I reacted too emotionally,' Lissa told him. 'I was too sensitive . . . too easily hurt and confused.' She got up to pick up the sweater she was knitting for Louise, and as she did so, stumbled against Joel's chair.

Instantly his hand shot out to steady her, his arm supporting her as she fell, so that somehow she ended up in his lap feeling both stupidly clumsy and flustered, but strangely enough with no desire to shrink away from him; with none of the tension she would have expected to feel.

'Lissa?'

She looked at him automatically, smiling herself when she saw the amusement lightening his eyes and curling his mouth. 'Do you suppose Louise is going to expect me to kiss you goodbye every morning?' he asked her in a lazy drawl.

The teasing amusement in his voice was familiar to her and she responded to it relaxing in the half circle of his arm, shrugging easily.

'Umm . . . well *I* suspect that she is,' he continued softly, 'and that being the case I definitely feel our technique could do with a little polishing.'

'I . . .' Whatever objection she had been about to make slid from her mind forever when Joel slid his fingers into her hair, their warmth spread across the back of her scalp, heating her skin, preventing her from moving; from avoiding the sensually slow downward movement of his head, as his lips feathered softly across her skin. First her temple, then the corner of her eye; the vulnerable hollow of her cheekbone where his breath against her ear, coupled with the slowly gentle movement of his fingers against her scalp, made her shiver with pleasure. With *pleasure*! Lissa acknowledged numbly, hearing him murmur her name and responding automatically to the sound of his voice so that she turned towards him unwittingly facilitating the warm glide of his mouth against her own.

She had been kissed before; and had even enjoyed those kisses, before she discovered the truth about herself, but this somehow was different. For a start no one had ever kissed her with such gentle thoroughness; such innate tenderness and yet somehow at the same time conveying that there was a potential within that tenderness for something deeper and far more dangerous. There was nothing intimidating or frightening about the way Joel's mouth moved on hers, and yet her body was aware with a deep nerve-tingling frisson of awareness that if she were to signal that she desired it there could be much, much more.

And she *did* desire it, Lissa acknowledged inwardly . . . Unbelievably she was tempted to slide her arms round Joel's neck and hold him closer, to press her body against his and feel it harden with masculine desire.

She wanted him to make love to her! Immediately she tensed and he let her go. Instinctively she veiled her eyes from him, frightened of what he might see in them; that he might guess what she was feeling. And what? she asked herself. Take advantage of it? Feel sorry for her? She scarcely knew which she disliked the most. Somehow she managed to scramble off his knee, and outside the inner turmoil of her thoughts she was aware of the sound of her own voice, high and tense, gabbling inanities about the time, desperately trying to provide a smoke-screen for her to hide behind.

She knew that Joel was studying her, watching her with unnerving narrow eyed scrutiny. What was he thinking? Why had he kissed her? If it had just been a game then it had been a cruel one, and somehow unlike the man she knew him to be.

'Lissa, sometimes I'll have to kiss you,' he said quietly at last. 'It's expected occasionally of married couples, even in these enlightened times.'

That drew a shaky smile from her, and he smiled too. 'Surely it wasn't so bad?' There was a whimsical quality to his smile that relaxed her.

'No, of course not.' So that was it. Joel was just trying to accustom her to the social kisses they might have to exchange, but there had been a warm persuasiveness in the movement of his mouth against hers that had reminded her that he was a powerfully virile man and so she said awkwardly, 'Joel . . . what will you do . . . what will happen . . .? You can't live the rest of your life in celibacy,' she managed at last.

'Lissa, I've got so much on my mind at the moment that there just isn't room for sexual frustration,' he told her drily. 'When there is . . .' He shrugged and then said tight-lipped, 'Well let's just say I won't burden you with it.'

The next morning Louise didn't have to remind Joel to kiss her. He bent automatically and dropped a light caress on Lissa's cheek as he got up from the table, and she told herself that it couldn't possibly be disappointment that coursed through her at the lightness of that brief, pre-occupied touch.

Joel was late coming home again. Louise pouted a little when she discovered that he wouldn't be there to read her bedtime story, but eventually settled down. In fact Lissa was delighted with the way both little girls had adapted to their new environment. Whenever Louise mentioned her parents Lissa made a point of talking to her about them, encouraging her to keep their memory alive without touching on the tragedy of their death. Louise seemed to have accepted the fact that they were gone from her life in the physical sense, although sometimes she betrayed a tendency to cling to either Joel or herself, Lissa acknowledged.

At eight o'clock Joel rang to say that he was on his way home. He sounded tired and yet good humoured. 'I've settled on someone for the Managing Directorship,' he told her. 'He starts next week.'

'Louise will be pleased,' Lissa told him. 'She was complaining tonight because you weren't here to read her story.'

Anyone listening to them would think them a long married couple, Lissa reflected when she replaced the receiver. But they were not married. Not in the real sense. What *would* Joel be like as a lover? Considerate, skilled, passionate . . .? Stop it she warned herself. Why was she continually exhibiting this desire to dance with danger . . . to flirt, even if it was only in the privacy of her own mind, with the idea of Joel as a lover?

Perhaps it was because the thought that he never

would be piqued her interest. But it wasn't pique alone that was responsible for the surge of physical awareness she felt whenever he was in the room.

She heard his car draw up as she was putting the final touches to their meal. He walked into the kitchen, surprising her with a brief kiss on her exposed nape, the way in which her bones turned to melting heat surprising her even more.

'Champagne,' he told her with a grin, showing her the bottle. 'I thought we'd celebrate the end of my career with Hargreaves International.'

Lissa laughed, catching his mood, banishing him from the kitchen while she finished what she was doing.

They had the champagne before dinner—and after it, and although Lissa demurred Joel insisted on her drinking some wine with her meal.

By the time she got up from the table she felt distinctly light-headed, but in such a relaxed carefree way that she couldn't refuse when Joel refilled her champagne glass. 'We've got to finish it,' he told her, 'otherwise it will go flat.'

The golden bubbles tickled her throat, sliding smoothly down it inducing a sensation of relaxed light-heartedness inside her. Even her blood seemed to be fizzing slightly. They talked, or at least Joel did, while she listened in a hazy cotton wool, other-worldly cloud of relaxation. Occasionally she had the impression that he was watching her . . . waiting for something . . . but she dismissed it as imagination. At ten o'clock she started yawning and when Joel suggested she go to bed she didn't demur.

'I'll clear these away,' he told her, indicating the

empty glasses. 'Sure you can manage?' he grinned as she stood up and promptly wobbled slightly.

'If you're suggesting that I'm tipsy, then you're quite right,' she told him, 'and what's more it's all your fault.'

'Want me to carry you upstairs, or can you manage on your own two feet?' He said it teasingly, and yet when he looked at her Lissa felt the most unexpected surge of desire kick upwards along her nervous system. She giggled nervously to conceal it and shook her head.

Once upstairs, she showered languidly, studying the smooth slickness of her wet skin as she stepped out and reached for a towel. Her body was something she rarely looked at as a rule, but tonight she found herself studying it, aware of a certain sensuality to it that she had never noticed before. Fleetingly she wondered if Joel still found her desirable, trying to dismiss the thought as she towelled herself dry and then slipped on her cotton nightie, but unable to do so. She was like a child, excited by the thought of playing with fire, even while she knew that parental rule protected her from doing so she thought, angry with herself, trying to shake off the languorous indolence of her movements.

She had just climbed into bed when Joel came in.

'I've brought you a nightcap,' he told her, handing her another glass. 'The last of the champagne. Drink it, it will help you sleep.'

The glass was three quarters full and Lissa sipped at it, watching him move about the bedroom. He took off his shirt and as though she were an observer to her own reactions she found herself monitoring her own physical response to him. His skin was faintly olive, tanned and sleek, his muscles hard without being over-developed. He disappeared into the bathroom, and Lissa heard the shower running.

She had just about finished her champagne when he came back and she watched him walk towards her.

'Finished?' As he got into bed beside her, he turned towards her and took her glass. She was still sitting up and as he turned away to put the glass on the tray his hand rested lightly on her shoulder preventing her from lying down. The bedside lamps were still on and as Lissa reached out to snap hers off, Joel reached across her, his arm a dark bar against the whiteness of her nightdress. For some reason Lissa seemed unable to take her eyes off it. Her light went out, Joel's arm moving against her body. Wonderingly she touched the olive skin of his forearm, completely absorbed in the sensation of his skin beneath her fingertips, warm and vital. She looked up at him, his face half in the shadow thrown by the other lamp. He leaned forward and his lips brushed hers. Curiously she was neither surprised nor apprehensive. It seemed as though some part of her mind had known that he was going to kiss her and directed her to turn into his kiss rather than away from it. His hand left the lamp and curled round her, turning her, but all her concentration was fixed on and fascinated by the slow movement of his mouth against her own and her own response to it. Easily, fluidly, she felt the natural reaction of her body to his proximity. Her mouth parted at the gentle insistence of his tongue, her senses half bewildered and totally confused by the delicately explorative way he ran it over her lips. She wanted more . . . more than this lightly arousing intimacy she realised inwardly, but that knowledge did not shock or frighten her. On the contrary, it seemed completely natural and right. So much so, that her hands lifted to Joel's neck, her lips parting yearningly for his kiss.

But he didn't kiss her. Instead he lay down, pulling her down on top of him, burying his face in her hair, tightening one arm round her waist while the thumb of his free hand, probed and stroked the vulnerable skin of her neck. Tiny frissons of pleasure shivered through her and while she knew Joel must be aware of them, she didn't feel ashamed or embarrassed, instead she arched closer to him, closing her eyes and abandoning herself to the shivering delight he was arousing.

'Lissa . . . Lissa, look at me.' His lips brushed lightly over her closed eyelids and dutifully she opened them drowning in the deep gold pools of his. He kissed her cheek, lightly, trailing tantalising kisses to the corner of her mouth. Lissa gave a small tormented moan. She wanted him to kiss her properly. Almost as though he knew how she felt his mouth touched hers. But the contact was too light . . . too fleeting. He kissed her again just as lightly and Lissa could feel the blood drumming frantically in her veins. Her fingers curled protestingly into his shoulder, her lips clinging pleadingly to his when he kissed her again. Her small moan of protest when the pressure she craved for was removed was checked as his mouth returned to hers, this time satisfying the hunger inside her. Lissa gasped, reality melting like snow in the desert sun. Suddenly nothing was more important than that Joel kept on kissing her as he was doing right now. When he slid her nightdress straps off her shoulder she shuddered in reaction to his fingers against her skin but it wasn't a shudder of rejection. How had she never known until now how right it would be to feel his hand against her breast, slowly stroking its rounded shape. She made a sound beneath his kiss, suddenly hating the intrusion of her cotton nightdress for coming between his touch and her skin, and when he released her mouth she tugged ineffectually at the fabric protesting huskily, 'It's in the way. Take it off.'

The hot glitter in Joel's eyes made her tremble, but in anticipation not fear, eager for the moment when he slid her nightdress from her body and cupped her breasts in his hands. Her heart was racing so fast it was making her dizzy, through a champagne induced cloud she gazed at Joel.

'Are you enjoying this, Lissa?' he asked huskily, 'Does it give you pleasure?'

Amazingly it did. She nodded her head slowly, watching the smile curl his mouth. 'So am I,' he told her softly. His mouth nuzzled her throat, finding and exploiting a thousand pleasure spots, his teeth nipping gently until she twisted and arched against him in heady abandon.

Beneath the slow caress of his hands her breasts swelled and ached, her nipples tight and hard, wanting something more than the lightly arousing brush of his thumb. When he bent his head and slowly dragged his tongue over the tightness of her nipple Lissa reacted instinctively, her finger-nails finding his spine and grating over the vertebrae until he shuddered. 'What is it you want, Lissa? This?' His mouth moved over her skin sending shock waves of arousal shuddering through her when it reached her nipple. In the light from the lamp she could see their entwined bodies; his dark and lean, hers feminine, curved, pale apart from the rosy aureoles of her breasts. Her nudity which hitherto had always displeased her was now something she took pleasure in. Joel's hand cupped her other breast, his head bending towards it and desire kicked to life inside her, her body arching into his possession. She felt almost faint from the pressure of needing him so much. She muttered his name watching him slowly releasing the swollen tip of her breast, her fingers curling into his hair as the need to feel his mouth against her breast again overwhelmed her.

'Lissa . . .' There was a raw, primitive message of need in the way Joel said her name, the fierce demand of his mouth on hers, enflaming her senses further. She trembled against his body, flattening her palms on his chest, confused by the harsh dragging cry that came from his throat when she did so. Beneath her hands she could feel the prickle of the dark hair that grew on his chest and also the tightness of his nipples. Were they as vulnerable to pleasure as her own? Slowly she bent towards them, running her tongue over their sharp outline as Joel had done with her. She felt his chest muscles contract as he dragged air into his lungs, his fingers curling into her hair.

'Oh God yes, Lissa. Yes . . . do that again.'

His abandonment excited her, the hoarse words of praise and demand that came from his throat inciting her to blindly follow his commands. There was pleasure to be found in touching as well as being touched she was discovering, especially when Joel's response to her left her in no doubts as to the way she aroused him.

'I'm the one who's supposed to be doing the seducing,' he whispered in her ear. 'Not you.'

He was still wearing his pyjama trousers and as her glance rested on them and then skittered away he released her rolling on to his side while he tugged them off, quickly coming back to her. The heat and power of the maleness of him against her skin was intensely arousing and Lissa clung to him.

Now dimly, as though the information were of little importance to her and somehow divorced from her she realised that had it not been for the champagne she had drunk she would not be here with Joel like this; that she would never have been able to put her fears and torturous self-doubts aside for long enough to allow him to touch and arouse her as he had, but somehow this knowledge was only of minor import.

Slowly Joel caressed her body, his touch magically conveying to her that while he was the one who was in control inciting and arousing the leaping pulses beating under her skin he too was also held in thrall paying homage to her femininity in the age old way of man; both master and slave to it.

In the shadowy half light she watched his fingers described dizzying seductive patterns of delight against her skin; the curve of her hip, her thigh . . . She closed her eyes shuddering achingly, clinging to him, crying out his name.

His mouth brushed hers, calming, comforting as

though he knew of the primaeval fear suddenly rushing through her body at the weight of his against it.

'Shush . . . relax . . .'

He was soothing her as he might have done Louise when she was in the grip of one of her nightmares Lissa realised but somehow it didn't matter, what did matter was that she clung to the reassuring calmness of his voice letting it strike at the deepest inner core of her. His mouth covered hers again and she clung to him letting the fierce need he was arousing inside her explode and drown out everything else. She was discovering within herself an intensely sensual streak that she now dimly perceived had perhaps always been there. Perhaps it was the very sensuality of her nature which had caused her to react so violently in the past. Her parents had been severely puritanical in their views; so much so that Lissa was beginning to see how her up-bringing must have been at war with much in her own nature.

'Are you enjoying this?'

Joel's question caught her off-guard. Before his near silence had added to the whole unreal aura that had enveloped her from the first moment he took her in his arms. Almost she had persuaded herself that she had strayed into some fantasy dream world from which she could simply wake up any time she wished, but now suddenly reality hit her. She *was* here . . . in Joel's arms, enjoying his lovemaking with an intensity that was sweeping away all her previous conceptions of herself.

As she looked into his eyes, seeing them clearly now, without the benefit of any champagne induced fogging haze; seeing within them a fine mingling of compassion, tenderness, and something else . . . something so eternally masculine and elemental that her body responded automatically to it, curving into his, her husky, 'Yes,' was half lost against his skin as she pressed her lips to his throat confused by the maelstrom of emotions suddenly seething within her, knowing that it was not purely desire that was making her so femalely pliable in his arms.

His skin tasted salt against her tongue and while part of her acknowledged the pleasure of such tactile contact her mind laboured dully trying to understand by what tortuous tracks and by-ways she had come to where she was now . . . to loving him. The admission that she loved him slid so easily into her mind that she knew it must have been there some time. Instinct screamed at her that to love him would only bring her pain, but held within his arms it was impossible to listen to instinct or caution. She kissed him, tasting his skin, losing herself completely in the joy of absorbing all she could of him into her senses feeling the suddenly accelerated thud of his heartbeat as his body responded to the touch of her hands and mouth.

Now when he touched her there was a hint of pagan savagery beneath his tenderness that drew a corresponding response from her; as though physically their bodies were communicating on a deeper more primitive level than their senses. There was nothing she wanted more than his ultimate and complete possession of her, in fact she wanted it so badly that she was the one to initiate it, moving arousingly against him, her hips writhing seductively against his in an age old dance of seduction, which made it all the more bitterly devastating when suddenly, for no reason she could think of, behind her closed eyelids the old vision of him danced, bitter and contemptuous, freezing her body into rigid agony at the moment of his possession, destroying the golden bubble of pleasure that had enclosed her.

'Lissa!'

She shuddered under the harshly abrasive way he said her name. 'It's all right . . . Open your eyes.'

Unbelievably she was obeying him, opening her tightly closed eyes to look despairingly into his.

'See, it's all right. Look at me, Lissa. Look at me . . .' His heart was still thudding erratically, sweat glistening on his skin, but the topaz eyes were nothing like the ones that had haunted her darkness, the curve of his mouth; the way his skin clung tightly to his cheekbones making her realise that the portrait relayed to her by her mind's eye was actually a caricature of reality . . . and that the way he was looking at her, with desire, with need . . . but most of all with understanding bore not the slightest resemblance to the expression she had once thought she had seen.

The muscles of her throat started to relax, her small choked sob of distress, silenced by the gentle pressure of his mouth.

'I want you, Lissa. I want to make love to you . . . to feel your body hold mine like a silken sheath . . .' He was interspersing his words with hungry, drugging kisses and she could feel herself responding, mentally and physically. 'I need to be deep inside you.' He moved as he spoke and her body melted, heat radiating outwards from deep inside her as he thrust against her and then inside her, her resistance flooding away on a shuddering breath of pleasure.

If she had thought she had already tasted the heady wine of pleasure, it had been a mere sip compared to what she was now experiencing. Once the trauma of her self-imposed barriers had been overcome the brief pain of Joel's initial possession had been nothing; something fleetingly felt and then forgotten beneath the waves of sensation which had overwhelmed her.

It was like touching heaven; being immortal . . . escaping the bonds of human limitations, and to know that Joel had shared that pinnacle of human pleasure with her made it all the more precious.

As her body relaxed into lethargy she summoned enough energy to say drowsily, 'You got me drunk deliberately didn't you?'

'Not drunk,' Joel corrected her, 'merely pleasurably relaxed. Do you regret it?'

Lissa shook her head. 'No.' How could she regret it? How could any woman regret sharing the most mystic of all human experiences with the man she loved? But then of course Joel did not *know* that she loved him, and he certainly did not love her. So why, why had he made love to her? Not just on impulse but deliberately. She turned towards him, studying his face in the lamp light. He looked relaxed, younger . . . supinely male and satisfied. A tiny thrill of pleasure ran through her. It was frightening to realise how vulnerable she was; how easily the smallest thing about him could please her, even to the extent of knowing that it was making love to her that had brought that almost animal langour to his body.

'I don't regret it at all Joel,' she told him honestly. 'But why? It wasn't just on impulse.'

'No,' he agreed. 'No it wasn't an impulse. Nor was it simply to satisfy my own desire for you. Oh yes,' he told her watching her, 'despite what you seem to have thought to the contrary; the fact that you were sexually inexperienced did not lessen my desire for you Lissa, and I'm not going to pretend that what we just shared together was anything less than extremely pleasurable . . . nor that I'm not hoping that it's a pleasure we will share again, but after you'd told me about your phobia it seemed to me that as I was the focal point of your trauma, then I should be the one to help you to overcome it. I thought if you could see me, not as some disapproving intruder, but as a man . . . a man very much aware of you as a beautiful and desirable woman, and every bit as vulnerable as you are yourself.' His thumb touched her cheekbone as she turned towards him. 'Yes, you are beautiful and desirable Lissa,' he repeated softly. 'Didn't my body tell you that?'

The memories conjured up by his words caused her to tremble slightly with a tiny thrill of remembered need.

'Yes,' she admitted huskily.

'It wasn't all entirely premeditated,' Joel added. 'The idea of getting you to relax via a few glasses of champagne only occurred to me today. I'd noticed that you didn't recoil quite as strongly from me when I touched you, so I knew you were beginning to relax with me.'

'But . . . but how did you know . . . that, that I'd be responsive to you?' Lissa asked him. Could he have guessed what she had not? Could he have known that she loved him. She hoped desperately that he did not. What he had said to her had made it plain that he did not love her; compassion and desire were not love.

'I didn't. It was a chance I had to take. For all I knew you could have been completely turned off by me physically, but I was hoping the champagne would lower your inhibitions for long enough for me to find out if that air of sensuality you have about you had any basis in reality. No matter what you might have been told, Lissa, one does not have to be wildly or passionately in love to enjoy a sexual relationship.'

'No, but surely love does add something,' she protested, remembering the surge of responsiveness she had felt when she realised that she loved him.

'A great deal,' he agreed, 'especially when we're talking about loving someone as opposed to being in love with them. You and I get on extremely well together Lissa . . . far better than I'd envisaged. It's my view that our marriage could be an extremely fulfilling and happy one—for both of us. Tonight was something of an experiment . . . an attempt on my part to make some reparation to you for the past. I felt I owed it to you to give you the freedom to overcome the past. I think I've succeeded, but now it's up to you to decide whether you wish to use that freedom in staying with me . . . as my wife . . . or whether you now feel you want to be free to form other relationships.'

Lissa knew that he was being completely fair and open with her but her heart ached for some whispered words of love . . . some absurd demand that she remain his and his alone, even if they were lies.

'Don't think about it now . . . Go to sleep.' As he switched off his lamp he asked teasingly, 'By the way, am I forgiven for my sins? Plying you with drink . . . seducing you?'

'I'll tell you in the morning,' Lissa responded drowsily. He wasn't going to have it all his own way. *She* might now know that she loved him, but it was a secret she would always keep to herself, she decided sleepily. Something she would do her utmost to conceal from him.

CHAPTER SEVEN

'LISSA!'

The shrill voice of her niece dragged Lissa from sleep. She opened her eyes tiredly to find Louise and Emma both next to her on the bed, still in their dressing gowns. Thin February sunlight streamed in through the windows, Joel's side of the bed empty. Her heart thudded in a mingling of fear and delight. She shivered slightly wondering if last night had actually happened or if it had all been a dream, and then she glanced at her watch, stunned to discover that it was gone ten. Why hadn't Joel woken her? Her skin grew warm as she pictured him waking up and watching her sleeping . . . while she was so vulnerable. It was just as well it was Saturday and that Joel did not have to go over to the factory.

'Uncle Joel is making breakfast,' Louise told her importantly. 'He said we were to let you sleep.'

'Yes, I did, didn't I?' Joel agreed wryly, walking in carrying a tray and putting it down on her bedside table. The rich aroma of the freshly made coffee was mouth-watering. He had also made some toast and the tray was set with a crisp white cloth and a small vase with some snowdrops. Lissa touched their pale fragile petals gently with the tip of her finger, tears stinging her eyes as she did so. She bent her head so that Joel wouldn't see them, but he lifted her chin with warm fingers and their eyes met. The warmth and tenderness in his held her. For a moment the earth seemed to tilt on its axis, her heart lurching, knocking against her ribs, and then he bent his head and kissed her lingeringly. A tremendous surge of joy welled up inside her, a happiness so intense that she shook with it. Louise clamoured for attention, Joel released her and the moment of intimacy between them was gone, but Lissa thought she would never forget that even though he might not love her he had cared enough to make that special gesture . . . to let her know in the cold light of morning that he still remembered the night and that he wanted her to remember it too.

Her mood of light-heartedness lasted all through the day. In the afternoon they took the girls shopping. Louise needed new shoes and of course Emma had to have some too. Once on she refused to be parted from them, and they left the shop amidst smiles from the assistants.

Because Joel had missed so many bedtimes during the week, Lissa organised a family tea, allowing the girls to stay up beyond their normal bedtime. While they were eating Joel talked about his plans to improve the bloodstock carried on one of the estate farms. His suave air of sophistication could be misleading Lissa reflected, remembering how awe-inspiring she had once found it. At heart he was very much a man who felt passionately about the land and everything connected with it. He was also extremely well read and interested in various aspects of the arts, especially music. All in all a complex, intelligent man with a hidden streak of sensitivity that would always endear him to the female sex. Fear brushed her heart leaving it thumping. Joel would always be attractive to other women. Had he loved her she had little doubt that he would remain faithful, but he didn't. What would happen if he ever met a woman that he did? How he would resent then his commitment to her . . . She couldn't bear it if that should happen. Stop it . . . stop it, she warned herself. She was crossing bridges she hadn't yet come to, dealing with problems before they arose.

They bathed the girls together, Louise clinging wetly to Lissa while she dried her, snuggling up to her and whispering, 'I love you, Lissa, do you love me . . .?'

Hugging her back, Lissa reassured her, suddenly aware that Joel was watching her.

'What is it?' she asked him, conscious of some slight withdrawal within him, some coolness that threatened her.

'Nothing.' He got up picking Emma up. 'I'll put this one to bed shall I?'

What had she done to make him withdraw from her like that? Lissa wondered. Had he perhaps thought looking at her of another woman . . . one who he might love as he did not love her?

As they prepared for bed Joel said casually, 'You know we're going to have to start doing some socialising shortly. People have left us alone knowing about John and Amanda's deaths, but I've had a couple of invitations recently to dinner, drinks, that sort of thing.'

He didn't say any more, but nor did he make any attempt to touch her once they were in bed, and although Lissa tried to reassure herself that there could be any number of reasons for the coolness she sensed within him she was filled with fear, experiencing for the first time in her life the full vulnerability that comes with love.

On Monday morning Mrs Fuller arrived, and it was soon quite obvious that the girls were going to take to her. Lissa was in Joel's study going through the post for him when the 'phone rang. She picked up the receiver automatically, not recognising the cool feminine voice on the other end of the line, explaining that Joel was out.

'Oh, I see. You must be John's sister-in-law then, Lisa . . .'

'Lissa,' Lissa corrected, feeling an inexplicable tug of antagonism towards the unknown caller. 'And actually I'm now Joel's wife.'

'Oh yes, of course, I'd forgotten he'd got married.' The excuse was smoothly bland, but Lissa was not deceived. Her caller had known all right and apprehension started to trickle down her spine. 'Joel is an old friend of my husband's,' the other woman continued. 'I was ringing to invite him round for dinner, but of course both of you must come. We normally get together once a month or so, but obviously because of the tragedy . . .'

They eventually fixed a date, Lissa's caller introducing herself as Marisa Andrews before she rang off.

Lissa knew little of Joel's friends apart from odd remarks he had made, and although commonsense told her it was ridiculous to feel that the other woman had deliberately set out to unnerve her, she still retained a distinct feeling that she had.

When Joel returned she told him about the 'phone call. He turned to look at the post, his back to her as he said, 'Marisa and Peter are old friends of mine. Peter and I were at university together. I was actually dating Marisa at the time and I introduced her to Peter.'

He didn't say anything else, but Lissa was conscious of an icy ache of depression that stayed with her all evening. When they eventually went to bed she deliberately turned her back to Joel, keeping well to her own side of the mattress. She thought she felt him touch her hair but she refused to turn round, and eventually the mattress shifted as he turned out his lamp. It was hours before she managed to fall asleep her mind churning sickly. Perhaps she was making a mountain out of a molehill . . . after all just because Joel had once dated this Marisa, it didn't mean she was the love of his life. Try to keep a sense of proportion she told herself but the fear would not go away and neither would the feeling that Joel had cooled towards her. He was still pleasant, but there was no warmth, no hint of teasing intimacy in the occasional duty kisses he gave her when he went out, and by Friday, Lissa was dreading the coming ordeal of Saturday's dinner party.

On impulse on Friday afternoon she asked Mrs Fuller if she would keep an eye on the girls, explaining that she wanted to buy a new dress. The housekeeper had already promised to look after them on the Saturday evening and Lissa had no qualms about leaving her with them. They enjoyed her company as much as she enjoyed theirs.

She had already been through her wardrobe and had found nothing there that would give her the confidence she felt she so badly needed, and so she decided she would go up to London. She arrived just after two and headed straight for Knightsbridge, determined to find herself a dress that would show the as yet unknown Marisa Andrews that she was no insignificant dreary little mouse. Joel had left the house that morning after breakfast saying that he had some business to conduct and not to expect him back until early evening. He hadn't said exactly where he was going and Lissa had found his unusual reticence chilling.

Trying to concentrate on the task in hand she hurried into Harvey Nicholls. Two hours later she emerged feeling light-headed with success and slightly guilty over the amount of money she had spent.

Her dress was very plain, long sleeved and high necked in fine wool crepe, fitting snugly over her waist and hips and then flaring out into a slightly bias cut skirt, but the simplicity of the design was more than compensated for in the rich dense blue colour of the fabric. It was a dress cut by a master hand for a woman who enjoyed being a woman and in it Lissa felt confidently sure of her femininity and appeal.

She had been lucky enough to get shoes to go with it, black suede with blue heels and satin ribbons, a touch of frivolity to offset the plainness of the dress.

She had just emerged into the street when she felt someone touch her shoulder. Swinging round she saw Simon Greaves.

'Good heavens . . . what a coincidence!'

'I've just been to see a potential client,' he told her. 'I couldn't believe it when I saw you. I thought you were immured in the depths of the country.'

'I came up to do some shopping.' It was hard to believe that she once thought herself attracted to him. Compared with Joel he seemed lacklustre somehow.

'Enjoying marriage are you?' There was a nasty little bite to the words, and Lissa was faintly surprised by it, but when he suggested they chat over a cup of coffee, she could think of no reason for refusing without being impolite and so she allowed him to guide her towards a small coffee house.

They were given a table in the window and once they had been served Simon started to ask her again how she had settled down in the country. He looked disbelieving when she said she was enjoying it, telling her, 'I got the distinct impression that you were being rather railroaded into this marriage. You know, Lissa, I miss you,' he added, covering her hand with his own. Since she could not snatch it away without causing a fuss, Lissa let it lie there, feeling her irritation towards him growing. 'Come back to my place this afternoon,' he cajoled. 'We can talk there.' The way he looked at her warned Lissa that talk wasn't all he had in mind and she felt instantly angry. Did he really think she was the sort of person who would contemplate breaking her marriage vows for something as shallow as a brief sexual fling? As she fought down her anger, she felt a prickle of awareness run down her spine. Someone was staring at her. She lifted her head and looked through the window. There was no one there. Shaking it she told herself that she would have to stop being so over-imaginative and then turned to tell Simon in no uncertain terms that she was not interested in what he was proposing. They parted less than amicably. A cold, frigid bitch, he had called her. Once she would have believed him, but now, thanks to Joel she knew better. Joel! Her heartbeat quickened as she thought about him, and suddenly she couldn't wait to get home. If only she knew what was making him so cool towards her. She froze almost in her tracks, other shoppers bumping into her. Dear God, what if Joel *had* guessed the truth. What if he suspected that she loved him and he was keeping her at a distance because he did not want any deep emotional involvement with her? She bit her lip in sudden anguish. Was that it? Had she stumbled on the truth? If so what was she to do? She could only play the game by Joel's rules, she decided as she made her way home. She would have to be as cool to him as he was to her so that he would not be burdened with an emotional commitment he obviously did not want. Unwanted love could be a burden and an embarrassment she acknowledged. Perhaps Joel feared that she would demand more of him than he could give and so had decided to hold himself aloof from her as a warning. She thought about the dress she had just bought with the express intention of showing herself off to her best advantage, and swallowed hard. She would have to pretend it was one she had had for some time. Pride stiffened her determination. From now on she would do nothing . . . nothing that would betray how she felt. She would be as cool and distant as Joel.

Luckily he was not in when she got back and she was able to take her purchases upstairs and put them away. He came in while she was watching the news on television, looking sombrely formal and almost chillingly forbidding. The expression on his face was close to the one of her nightmares, and her heart quailed as she looked at him.

'Busy day?'

'Yes . . . And you?'

Were they really reduced to this . . . to these banalities, she wondered miserably, contrasting them with the discussions and conversations they had shared with such enthusiasm not so very long ago.

'No . . . not really.' She wasn't going to tell him about her trip to London. He would want to know why she had gone, and that was something she wasn't going to tell him now.

She looked across at him, dismayed by the coldness in his eyes, conscious of a leashed tension about his movements. Was it purely because of her, or was it something to do with the fact that tomorrow they were dining with his old girl friend?

'I'm going out.'

The harsh anger in his voice cut coldly through her frail defences, chilling her and she shivered.

'When will you be back.'

'I don't know.' The curt dismissal in his voice hurt.

'What about dinner?'

'If I'm not here then start without me,' he told her derisively, striding towards the door, slamming it on his way out. She listened to his footsteps dying away and then the sound of his car engine firing, standing tensely where he had left her until that too faded. She then went into the kitchen pinning a bright smile to her face as she greeted the girls and Mrs Fuller.

Louise wanted to know where Joel had gone.

'He had to go and see someone about business,' she told the little girl, wondering as she did so, rather bleakly, how many times in the months and years to come she was going to repeat that phrase.

The physical consummation of their marriage, the tenderness Joel had shown her then, which should have boded so well for their marriage seemed only to have widened the gap between them.

Feeling thoroughly depressed Lissa went upstairs into her bedroom and opened her wardrobe door staring miserably at the blue dress she had bought with such fervent determination to draw Joel's attention to her.

Joel did return in time for dinner but he was withdrawn, curt to the point of aggressiveness whenever she talked to him so that gradually her questions ceased and a tense silence filled the room.

She was not surprised, rather relieved in fact, when after dinner Joel announced that he had work to do and disappeared in the direction of his study.

Lissa went to bed early but it was gone one when Joel came up, walking into the bedroom so quietly, not switching on any of the lights, so that she was forced to the conclusion that he would prefer her to be asleep. Her heart ached with love and despair.

Tomorrow was another day, and somehow she must find the courage to face it—and Marisa Andrews.

CHAPTER EIGHT

No one could ever have dressed for a dinner party with less enthusiasm Lissa thought miserably as she brushed her hair. Joel was in their bathroom; she could hear him splashing about under the shower. Disturbing mental images of the lithe maleness of him tormented her, making her hands shake so much that she had to put down the brush. Her body now awakened to the pleasure of Joel's lovemaking seemed to crave it with all the single minded intensity of an addict for his favourite drug. Whenever he was in the same room with her she ached with a tension that had nothing to do with tiredness or over-stretched nerves. It was humiliating that she should feel like this. How could she love and want him to this extent especially when she knew that he cared little or nothing for her?

He came out of the bathroom while she was zipping up her dress. Out of the corner of her eye Lissa studied him, tiny shivers of awareness feathering down her spine as he shrugged off his robe and started getting dressed. Unlike her he seemed totally unselfconscious about his nudity; totally unaware of the dry-mouthed anguish with which she fought not to look at him because to look was to want to touch and to go on touching . . .

Her zipper stuck and she made a small impatient sound. Joel looked up and frowned, immediately perceiving what had happened.

'Here let me.' His voice was as cool as the touch of his fingers against her over-heated skin. She could smell the clean male scent of him and she wanted nothing more than to turn round and be taken into his arms. The intensity of her own emotions overwhelmed her making her tense her body against any such betrayal.

'Relax.' The cool bite in Joel's voice chilled her. 'I'm not about to rape you, if that's what's worrying you.'

Painful colour stung her skin as she caught the cynically bitter undertones to his voice. 'I didn't think you were.'

Her zip came free and slid smoothly upwards. Joel stepped away from her, turning his back on her as he continued dressing. He looked devastatingly masculine in the formality of his evening clothes, Lissa acknowledged miserably, watching covertly as he inserted gold links into his shirt cuffs, deftly snapping them closed.

'Ready?'

His glance swept over her, dismissing her without comment, his indifference towards her so painful that her face felt stiff from the effort of trying to conceal her feelings from him.

They went downstairs together, Joel's attitude towards her punctiliously correct as he handed her into the car.

As he started the engine he inserted a cassette into the tape deck, turning up the sound just loudly enough to make conversation difficult, effectively shutting her off from him Lissa thought. He couldn't have made it more plain if he had spelled it out for her, how uninterested in her he really was.

It took just under an hour for them to reach the Andrews' house—a rather solid Victorian red-brick building on the outskirts of a small village. The gateposts and short drive were illuminated clearly enough for Lissa to have a brief glimpse of the edge of an immaculate lawn that somehow matched the mental picture she had already built up of Marisa Andrews—cool, immaculate, perfectly groomed.

Joel stopped the car and released his seat belt, Lissa doing the same. She was out of the car before he could help her, and he gave a rather grim smile as he waited for her to precede him up the shallow flight of stone steps.

The door was opened before they rang. 'Joel, darling, I thought I recognised your car.'

Lissa recognised the smoothly feline feminine voice instantly. She could feel the tiny hairs on the surface of her skin prickling with atavistic dislike. 'Do come in, both of you.'

As Lissa walked into the hall ahead of Joel she had ample opportunity to study their hostess, as Joel bent to kiss her cheek. Small, much smaller than herself, ash blonde hair cut to emphasise the delicacy of her features; she was everything that she herself was not Lissa recognised on a downward plunge of her heart. Although she suspected that her hostess must be somewhere in her early thirties, she could easily have passed for a woman of twenty-seven or eight. Although she tried not to, Lissa couldn't help but be aware of the way Marisa's fingers clung to Joel's shoulder, as she prolonged his greeting kiss, neither could she miss the look of cold malevolence which her hostess directed towards *her* as she cooed with soft sweetness, 'Joel darling, you're neglecting your new wife. Do please introduce her to me.'

Grimly Lissa listened to Joel's introductions, hating the tinklingly false laugh Marisa gave when she interrupted gaily, 'Oh Joel, no need to be quite so formal. Joel and I have known one another for years,' she told Lissa, directing a coquettish glance towards Joel. 'You know darling, you've grown into such an impossibly handsome man, that I really think perhaps I should have married *you* and not Peter. But then handsome men always make difficult husbands, don't they Lissa? One always has to be on one's guard in case one loses them to someone else, wouldn't you agree Lissa? Far better I always think to be a handsome man's mistress than his wife. So much more fun.'

Lissa managed a cool smile, knowing quite well that Marisa was trying her best to make her feel uncomfortable and outside the charmed circle she had so plainly drawn around Joel and herself.

'Where's Peter?' Joel enquired easily. 'I haven't seen him for ages.'

'Oh he's in the drawing room.' Marisa pulled a face. 'He's watching some stuffy programme on high finance. It should be over soon. My husband's a stockbroker,' she explained to Lissa, 'and sometimes I think he cares more about his stocks and shares than he does about me.'

'Impossible,' Joel replied smiling at her. 'Or at least if he does, then he's a fool.'

Lissa could feel the anger inside her, heating to a white-hot glow as she observed this interchange. Her nails were pressing so hard into the palms of her hands that they hurt.

The proprietorially flirtatious manner Marisa

had adopted towards Joel set the tone for the whole evening, and Lissa had to grit her teeth and pretend not to notice the number of times her hostess excluded her from the conversation by referring to events which had happened in the past. She also had to pretend not to notice how often Marisa managed to touch Joel, or to draw his attention to her. To counteract her hostess's rudeness, Lissa directed her attention towards Peter Andrews, who despite his rather solid appearance had a keen, rather dry wit, which he exercised to their mutual enjoyment.

'Old Joel married,' Peter murmured jovially when they had reached the coffee stage. He directed a brief grin towards his friend and added, 'I was beginning to think I'd never see the day.'

'Oh come on darling, be practical,' Marisa interrupted. 'Naturally Joel had to marry. After all he has those children to think of now . . .'

As she waited for Joel to at least make a token attempt to deny Marisa's insinuation Lissa could feel her face burning with humiliation and resentment. How dare he subject her to Marisa's bitchiness? How dare he bring her here to be insulted and tormented by the sight of Marisa continually making it plain how much she wanted him?

Peter gave an embarrassed cough and glanced rather uncertainly towards Lissa.

Pride came to her rescue. With a brittle smile she said tightly, 'That's right Marisa. The children are Joel's responsibility and as I've discovered, he's a man who takes his responsibilities extremely seriously, but of course, taking our marriage seriously doesn't preclude either of us from . . .' she managed a tiny, expressive shrug, 'shall we say making other friendships outside that marriage.'

There was a definite silence when she had finished. Without looking at either Joel or Marisa she picked up her coffee cup and made a pretence of drinking. Let Marisa make what she liked of that, she thought viciously.

'Goodness. How very . . . civilised of you,' was Marisa's eventual comment. She turned to Joel. 'Darling I must say that had you married me, I'm afraid I wouldn't have been anything like as practical, and how you must have changed.' She directed Lissa a smile of sweet malice. 'You perhaps won't believe this, but I remember Joel as being quite outrageously possessive and jealous.'

'Yes, I'm sure,' Lissa agreed with commendable control, and an acidly sweet smile of her own, 'but that was a long time ago wasn't it? I think everyone feels things more intensely in their late teens and early twenties. I know I did.'

The evening dragged on interminably. Marisa insisted on taking Joel into her own private sitting room to show him some prints she had recently bought, and to judge by the willingness with which Joel went with her, she had been right to suspect that Joel still cared for her. Why had Marisa married Peter when it was so obvious that she preferred Joel, Lissa wondered miserably. Had she perhaps married Peter on some impulsive whim only to discover that it was Joel she really wanted?

'You mustn't mind Marisa,' Peter told her, breaking in on her thoughts. 'I'm afraid she's grown rather used to thinking of Joel as her exclusive property.'

'No, of course not,' Lissa agreed, feeling rather sorry for him. 'I realise that you're all very old friends.'

'Yes ... Joel was dating Marisa when he introduced her to me,' Tony agreed confirming what Joel himself had told her. 'Of course, he wasn't in a position to get married then. His father was extremely strict with him—kept him on a very tight rein financially.'

Lissa bit her lip. Was that the reason Marisa had married Peter in preference to Joel? Because Peter had been the better-off financially. Lissa was under no illusions about the other woman. Marisa was a woman who wanted the very best that life had to offer. Her marriage to Peter had given her financial security, but now she wanted more ... she wanted Joel ... And Joel quite plainly wanted her, Lissa reflected sickly seconds later as they both walked into the room. There was still a faint smear of lipstick on Joel's mouth, and she felt the sickness boil into fierce hatred as she averted her eyes from Marisa's cat-like expression of complacency.

It was gone one in the morning when they eventually left. The angry surge of adrenalin which had kept Lissa going throughout the evening evaporated the moment she got into the car, leaving her unbelievably exhausted and more miserably unhappy than she could ever remember being in her life.

They had driven half a dozen miles or so when the tape finally stopped. As Lissa reached out to turn it over, Joel stopped her, his eyes meeting hers briefly for a moment, before he bit out, 'And just what the hell were you trying to do to Marisa?'

What was *she* trying to do to *her*! Lissa took a deep breath and tried to steady herself, her voice when she eventually managed to speak sounded unfamiliar, but reassuringly steady. 'Only the most stupid or appallingly cruel man would confront his wife with his mistress in such intimate conditions,' she told him huskily. 'If I was rude to Marisa, then I was only responding to her verbal attacks on me.'

For a moment it seemed to Lissa that he checked and would have said something, but then he paused and at last said coolly, 'In self-defence? Is that all it was? There were one or two moments when I thought I detected more than a hint of jealousy.'

His astuteness infuriated her. 'Me, jealous of your relationship with Marisa? Why did she marry Peter and not you in the first place Joel? Was it because he promised to be the better husband from a material point of view?'

He stopped the car with a jerk that threw her forward in her seatbelt with such force that her head almost bumped into the windscreen. The jolt winded and shocked her, but Joel made no allowances for that, his hands gripping her shoulders as he swung her round to face him, his eyes glittering with a savagery that made her draw in her breath. He did love Marisa. He would never have reacted like this otherwise. Pain . . . awful and all-consuming filled her until there was no room for anything else, not even the ability to be alarmed by the quality of his anger.

She let what he was saying wash over her, and then when he had finished said numbly, 'You've still got her lipstick on your mouth . . .'

She watched in anguish as he raised his hand and rubbed it off.

'Even if you didn't care about humiliating me, Joel,' she said tiredly as he re-started the engine, 'I should have thought you might have spared some consideration for Peter. After all he is supposed to be your friend.'

'Peter knew what he was getting into when he married Marisa,' Joel informed her harshly.

After that neither of them spoke until they reached Winterly. Lissa got out of the car quickly and went straight upstairs to the girls' room. Mrs Fuller had promised to listen out for them, but they were both fast asleep. Emma was sucking her thumb, Lissa released it from her mouth, and bent down to kiss both girls, tears stinging her eyes. Joel had married her for their sake; and she must always bear that in mind. The tender, caring lover she thought she remembered had just been an illusion. Now, she had no idea why Joel had made love to her. Once she had thought she knew, but after tonight ... She shuddered suddenly picturing him with Marisa ... the sickness grew inside her and she dashed into the girls' bathroom. Joel walked in just as she was wiping her face, frowning quickly.

'Something wrong?'

'I must have eaten something that disagreed with me,' Lissa told him shakily, snapping off the light. 'I think I'll go to bed now Joel. I'm tired.'

'Of me? Is that what that little speech to Marisa about marriage was all about?'

He followed her into their room and tugged savagely at his shirt buttons, stopping suddenly to frown and walk over to his tallboy. He opened a drawer and took out a long flat gift-wrapped package, which he tossed casually over to her. 'I nearly forgot, today's your birthday, isn't it?'

Lissa could have wept. It was, and she herself had almost forgotten about it. She would rather have had no present at all from Joel than one thrown at her in this careless manner which made it plain that it was no more than a duty gift.

'Aren't you going to open it?'

She did so reluctantly with fingers that trembled, unable to suppress a small gasp of surprise when she opened the slim box and discovered the pearl choker inside.

'I...' She didn't know what to say to him. Tears misted her vision, swimming in front of her eyes. She touched the pearls gently, and wished that he was giving her this gift with love and caring.

'They're beautiful.'

'I bought them because the texture and sheen reminded me of your skin.'

Her eyes opened wider, her head lifting until her glance met his, the visions conjured up in her mind by his quiet words making her go hot with need. If she closed her eyes she could almost imagine he was touching her, caressing her with the slow intensity she remembered so vividly, learning the contours of her body, absorbing her into himself as though he never wanted to be apart from her.

'I...'

'I went up to London to get them the other day,' he continued quietly, but now there was a new note to his voice, a grim bitterness that caught her attention. She frowned and he laughed harshly, 'Yes that's right ... the day you also decided to visit the city. Why did you go there Lissa? Or can I guess? Was the temptation to see Greaves too much to resist. Did you want to see what effect you would have on him now that you're free to take him as your lover? Did you Lissa? Did you let him take you back to his flat and make love to you?'

Lissa could only stare at him. Joel had seen her with Simon! She remembered now that she had felt as though someone had been watching her when they were sitting in the café. The words of explanation and denial trembled on the tip of her tongue, and then she remembered Marisa.

'Is that why you made it so obvious tonight that Marisa is your mistress, Joel,' she countered with commendable coolness. 'Because you saw me with Simon?'

'So you don't deny it?'

He was watching her with menacing intensity, the glittering rage so clearly discernible in his eyes igniting a strange mixture of misery and exhilaration inside her which spurred her on to ignore the warning signs.

'Why should I? Do you deny that Marisa is your mistress? If *you* are free to enjoy a sexual relationship with someone else, then why should I not be?'

'If it's sex you want, then I can satisfy that need for you right here and now.'

Too late she realised her mistake. Lissa backed away hastily, the box containing her pearls clattering on to the carpet. Common sense told her to face Joel and tell him quite simply that it was all a stupid mistake, and that far from encouraging Simon to make sexual advances towards her, she had been telling him quite categorically that she didn't want him, but something deeper than common sense took hold of her. She turned to run, motivated purely by blind, unthinking instinct. Joel caught her before she reached the door, swinging her round and into his arms, tightening them round her until she could feel the buttons of his shirt pressing into her. Even to breathe hurt, and although she twisted desperately against him she couldn't break free. One hand tangled in her hair, tugging painfully on the roots forcing her mouth to accept the bruising pressure of his. He kissed her with a sexual savagery that shocked her, and yet beneath her fear and anger ran an undeniable thread of liquid pleasure; a fierce need to match fire with fire and to respond to him with all the aching need that was building up inside her. It was hard to fight against herself and him, and even while she told herself that this was not right; that any intimacy between them while he was in this savagely punishing mood could only lead to further unhappiness for her, she could feel her will to resist slipping away from her. It was no use telling herself that he was simply using her as a vent for his frustrations and anger . . . that afterwards she would only feel renewed self-contempt and loathing . . . that by responding to him she was endangering her own self-respect. Her mouth softened under his, her heart thudding with delirious release as he recognised her surrender and took swift advantage of it, his tongue impatiently seeking access to her mouth, and when granted it, using her weakness ruthlessly against her. His fingers found her zipper and slid it down. Lissa was dimly conscious of his hands against her skin, smoothing up over her back, making her shiver first with pleasure and then with need as he pushed her dress away from her body. She was touching him too, sliding her hands inside his shirt, re-discovering the contours of his body. His mouth left hers, burning hotly against her skin as he tilted her head back, devastating her senses as he slowly ravaged the taut column of her throat.

'Is this what you want Lissa?' His fingers sought the clasp of her bra, freeing her breasts to his knowing touch. She managed a strangled protest that died away into a whimpering admission of pleasure as his lips followed his hands, the movement of his tongue roughly erotic as it brushed the sensitive peaks of her breasts. Her fingers bit protestingly into his shoulders, a fierce surge of pride and anger that he could do this to her making her fight against the sexual coercion he was using so cold bloodedly. He made a harsh sound of pain but far from releasing her pushed her down on to the bed, following her there. Momentarily her hands were free, and Lissa used them to fend him off, anger turning swiftly to fear when her nail accidentally caught his shoulder, tearing his flesh. Joel swore, swiftly imprisoning both her hands, pinning them above her head. A wild reckless sexual excitement thundered through her as she saw his expression and read in his eyes the same fierce hunger that was in her own. Joel wanted her! It was savagely satisfying to know that even though he loved Marisa she could make him want *her*. She wanted to taunt him with her knowledge to humiliate and denigrate him as he had done her. He moved against her, expelling a deep breath, and she caught sight of the thin thread of blood against his skin where she had scratched him. His glance followed hers. Their eyes meshed, his burning dark metallic gold, hers a dark bright, defiant hazel. She could feel the hard muscles of his thighs against her body . . . she knew that he wanted her . . . This should have been her moment of triumph, her chance to show him that he was not invincible. He moved slightly and her eyes were drawn back to his shoulder. Almost absently she touched his skin with her tongue, feeling him flinch and tense. His blood tasted slightly rusty, the knowledge that she had caused it to flow turning her bitterness to guilt. What if at this moment he did want her? Wasn't he only really using her as an escape valve because he couldn't have the woman he really loved? The fight went out of her, leaving her empty . . . drained. She felt Joel's grasp of her wrists slacken and prepared to move away from him. His hand cupped her face and she turned to look at him, dreading the words of contempt she was sure she was going to hear. As she looked into his eyes the expression glittering back at her there was one she didn't recognise. His skin seemed to be drawn too tightly over his bones, a dark flush staining it.

'Lissa.' He said her name in a thickly unfamiliar voice. 'Do that again,' he commanded, moving so that her mouth was pressed against his shoulder. A deep shudder ran right through him as she automatically complied, touching his skin with her tongue with nervous delicacy, stunned that such a brief physical contact should apparently have so much power to move him. His hand found her breast, his thumb rubbing urgently against her swollen nipple. Lissa forgot that he didn't love her, silencing her moan of anguished desire against the warm flesh of his throat. She felt his body surge against her own and recklessly arched up against him prolonging the tingling contact. Joel bent his head, his mouth fiercely claiming the aroused peak of her breast, his fingers caressing its twin.

Lissa arched and writhed beneath him, her nails raking helplessly against his skin, desire exploding tumultuously inside her as Joel continued to arouse spirals of unbearable delight inside her, tiny darts of fire running shuddering through her body from its point of contact with the fierce heat of his mouth.

'You're my wife, Lissa.' He said it thickly, against her skin, whether as a reminder that he had every right to make love to her if he chose, or as an explanation for the fact that he was doing so, she didn't know. She ought to stop him, to remind him that he didn't love her, but her treacherous body ached too much for the sweet agony of consummation. When he removed the rest of their clothing she didn't stop him, simply watching him silently. Shadows made a subtle play of shading against his skin, one moment soft gold the next bronze. She ached to touch him Lissa acknowledged, watching him as he bent over her, removing her underclothes.

A slight shiver ran through her as his hand brushed her hip.

'Cold?'

She shook her head as his hand curled round the spot he had just touched. He was kneeling beside her, and when she first felt the light brush of his tongue where his hand had rested she thought she must be imagining it. Her head lifted and swivelled round and she gasped as she felt the brief caress again. Her skin quivered responsively where he had touched it, darting quick-silver thrills of pleasure running from nerve ending to nerve ending. She could hardly believe it when Joel bent his head and slowly started to drag his tongue over the slight swell of her stomach. She jerked away from him in helpless torment, but he imprisoned her against the bed, his hands holding the narrow bones of her hips, while his tongue left quivering trails of moist destruction over her skin.

Lissa was completely powerless to stop him, and after a while she no longer wanted to try, held thrall to the swift, leaping fires of pleasure that burned inside her. At first she twisted helplessly from side to side as much in an attempt to escape the devastation of her senses as to avoid Joel's skilfully delicate touch, but all her struggles seemed to do was to give him access to areas of her skin that seemed even more responsive to him than the others had been.

'Joel what are you doing?' she managed to demand huskily at one point, tensing agonisingly as his tongue described a slow circle round her navel and then dipped tormentingly to explore its slight indentation.

'Just trying to keep you warm,' he replied suavely, 'you are getting warm aren't you Lissa?' he tormented softly.

Warm? She was burning up, her skin on fire.

By the time Joel's slow devastation of her body had reached her breasts she was shivering helplessly, aching for the full consummation of his possession. He kissed the tender fullness of their curves with mind-destroying slowness until Lissa couldn't hold back the fevered protest that left her lips. Once that final wall in her defences had been breached she couldn't keep silent her agonised pleas for him to end her torment, shattering the thick silence of the night, until Joel reached up and silenced her by pressing his finger against her mouth. Her lips parted, her tongue running frantically over the tips of his fingers, until driven half mad by the slow drift of his mouth against her breast she sucked feverishly on his fingers.

Dimly she was aware of Joel groaning, of him shifting his weight so that his body lay between her thighs, his lips exploring her throat, in between muttering hoarse words of praise and enticement against her skin. He withdrew his fingers from her mouth, brushing the outline of her lips with his thumb, lifting his head to look deeply into her eyes, his hands moving slowly down over her body, lifting it into his own.

Lissa shivered, trembling with aching desire. 'Tell me you want me more than you wanted him,' Joel demanded softly, watching her.

For a moment Lissa's mind was completely blank, and then when she realised the truth she could have wept with anguish. Joel had done this to her, aroused her to a pitch where her need for him was a throbbing ache that threatened to consume her, simply because his pride demanded that she want him more than she wanted Simon. If only he knew!

'Tell me!'

His face blurred for a moment as she blinked away tears. 'I want you more than I want Simon, Joel,' she said shakily at last. 'Much more.'

It was after all no less than the truth, and what he had done to her diminished him as much as it did her. Her body which had ached and hungered for his possession felt curiously drained of all feeling as he moved slowly and skilfully within her, rather like an overwound toy that was now broken, Lissa thought hazily, conscious of an overwhelming desire to break down and cry. Where she had ached for physical fulfilment now she ached for an emotional commitment to match her own. She heard Joel swear and then withdraw from her, but she was feeling too numb and lacerated to react.

'Lissa . . . what's wrong?' There was a raw uncertainty in Joel's voice that made her want to reach out and comfort him, but something stopped her. Joel didn't want *her*, he wanted Marisa. She felt her heart harden and shrink into a block of ice.

'Lissa!'

The tone of his voice demanded a response, but all she could manage was a flat, 'Using substitutes doesn't seem to work, does it Joel?' before she slid down into a yawning black void of nothingness.

CHAPTER NINE

SHE was violently ill when she woke up in the morning—a sure sign that she must have eaten something that disagreed with her Lissa thought as she washed and dressed.

Joel was up already, and mentally thanking God that she did not have to face him she made her way downstairs. They could not go on the way they were, last night had shown her that. What had happened to the compassionate tender man she had briefly known? She went into the kitchen, grimacing when she caught the smell of bacon and eggs.

Mrs Fuller looked at her in concern.

'Are you all right?'

'Just a little queasy,' Lissa explained, 'Something I ate, I expect.'

The housekeeper grinned at her. 'If you say so.'

It was several seconds before the import of her teasing remark sank into Lissa's consciousness. When it did, she went pale and sat down heavily on one of the chairs, staring blankly at the wall. Dear God she hadn't thought of that! What if she should be pregnant?

Impossible! Hardly, an inner voice taunted her—in fact it was all too probable. She had simply never thought about using any form of birth-control. It had never been necessary. While she was trying to come to terms with her shock, Joel and the girls walked in. All three of them looked healthily windblown, their cheeks glowing, Emma on Joel's shoulder, while Louise clung to his hand.

'Joel said we were to let you rest,' Louise announced, releasing Joel to run over to Lissa, clambering on to her knee and cuddling into her. She was discovering in her elder niece a very deep need to exhibit her affections physically, and Lissa responded to her unspoken plea for reassurance, hugging and kissing her.

'We went for a walk,' Emma announced as Joel placed her in her high chair.

Mrs Fuller served them breakfast, and Lissa felt relieved when she was simply given two slices of dried toast. Joel raised his eyebrows.

'I'm not hungry,' Lissa told him hastily, avoiding his eyes, and grateful for the housekeeper when she kept silent, merely exchanging a thoughtful glance with her over Joel's downbent head. She had dreaded facing him this morning after the way she was sure she must have betrayed herself to him last night, but now she had something even more worrying on her mind. What on earth would she do if she was pregnant?

Stop thinking about it she cautioned herself, it's probably nothing . . . too much rich food last night. She ought to have been reassured, but somehow she was not.

When he looked at her again there was a strange bitter tension in his eyes, a tightness to his mouth that took her back to that night almost ten years ago. Unknowingly she flinched, pushing her plate away, shivering slightly, aware of Joel getting up and coming towards her, and almost cringing away from him as he did so. How could she bear to have him touch her now when she knew that every time he did, it was another woman he had in his heart.

The 'phone rang shrilly, the sound harsh and challenging. Joel frowned, glanced at her, and then walked across the kitchen to pick up the receiver. Once he had moved away from her Lissa was conscious of an easing of the constriction in her muscles. Louise and Emma were both far too young yet to be aware of the strained atmosphere between the adults, but Mrs Fuller must have noticed it. If only she had known about Marisa before she agreed to marry Joel! Even loving him as she now admitted she did, she would not have done so. While she had thought there was no other woman in his life she had hoped, ridiculously no doubt, that somehow a miracle would occur and Joel would eventually turn to her with more than mere physical desire and compassion.

Compassion! She checked a bitter little laugh. There had been precious little of that between them these last few days. In fact if she hadn't seen that other side of him she would never have believed it existed.

'Lissa.'

She turned at the sound of Joel's voice, abrupt and grim. 'It's for you,' he told her, holding out the receiver. 'Guess.'

Simon? Ringing her, but why, Lissa wondered, automatically getting up and walking over to the 'phone.

Joel moved away the moment she reached him. He looked angry, she noticed, his mouth compressed. A spurt of defiant anger welled up inside her. If it was permissible for him to have his affair with Marisa then what right had he to look so annoyed simply because another man telephoned her.

She turned her back on him, holding the receiver close to her ear.

'Lissa is that you?'

'Yes Simon.'

'Look, I'm just ringing to apologise for the other day. I know I was out of line.'

Lissa listened absently to his apologies, conscious all the time of Joel's presence in the room.

'How about lunch one day just to show that I'm forgiven,' Simon suggested.

'Lunch?' Lissa turned round and met the coldly condemning look in Joel's eyes. She took a deep breath. 'Yes, why not,' she agreed gaily. 'I'll give you a ring, shall I?'

They chatted for several more minutes, although when she eventually replaced the receiver, she couldn't have said what they talked about. A feeling of almost frightening exhilaration had lifted her out of her previous misery, and she knew it came from knowing that at least if she did not have the power to move Joel to love, she could move him to anger. She was flirting with danger, she warned herself as she sat down again, avoiding Joel's eyes, but why not? Joel didn't want her himself . . . so why should he get angry because he thought someone else did.

She already knew the answer to that question Lissa reminded herself.

Joel had made it plain enough when they married that he expected and intended to have her fidelity. But then she had expected something in return from him. Not love perhaps, but loyalty at least . . . an attempt to preserve the fiction that they had married because in part he cared for her. She had not expected to have his mistress flaunted openly in front of her without any show of concern about how she might feel.

She had half expected Joel to tackle her about Simon's 'phone call, but in the event he said nothing, and somehow that was worse.

As the days passed Lissa had the distinctly unpleasant sensation of something hanging ominously over her, a sensation too uncomfortably reminiscent of her childhood for her to bear it easily. She was also still suffering from nausea, and an acute nervous tension, which she knew she was communicating to Louise. The little girl had become clinging and petulant, and while Lissa fully understood and sympathised with her insecurity, the constant succession of broken nights they were enduring with Louise's recurrent nightmares were beginning to take their toll on her. Joel was so cold and distant towards her that she could hardly believe that they had ever really been lovers. He spent far more time away from the house, often going out in the evening and returning late. Lissa never questioned him as to where he had been, her stubborn pride refusing to allow her to let him see how much he was hurting her.

One week went by and then another. She had lost weight and there were dark circles under her eyes. Mrs Fuller who could not have failed to notice the atmosphere that existed between Joel and herself, and his constant absences, said nothing, but Lissa was acutely aware of her silent sympathy. It struck her that being a local Mrs Fuller might be quite aware of Joel's relationship with Marisa, and that too stung her pride.

She had intended to start Louise at playschool, but she herself felt far too lethargic to do anything about it. The last week in March, the temperature suddenly dropped several degrees, and Joel, for once appearing for dinner remarked that he felt they could expect snow. He frowned slightly as he said it, and Lissa guessed he was thinking of the safety of the stock.

Lissa had never realised until these last few weeks how lonely and cold a double bed could be when it was shared with a man one loved who felt nothing but indifference tinged with anger in return.

'Are you . . . are you planning on going out again tonight?' She wished she hadn't voiced the impulsive question when he frowned. For a moment she thought he didn't intend to reply and then he said suavely, 'Why, had you got something planned yourself?'

His blatant indifference and coldness towards her defeated her. She wanted to talk to him, to plead with him to discuss the state of their marriage and what future if any he envisaged for them. The sudden change in his attitude towards her was still something she hadn't really come to terms with. There were days when she felt completely muddled, unable to understand why he had changed from the tender considerate lover to whom she had given her heart and body to this cold, withdrawn man he was now. Maybe it was because he felt guilty about making love to her, seeing it as a betrayal of his love for Marisa? Maybe it was as she had orignally thought, that he feared she would read into his lovemaking a greater emotional commitment than he was prepared to give her. Either way there was only one way she would learn the truth and that was for him to tell her, but he continually blocked all her attempts to talk seriously to him on any subject other than the children. What hurt almost more than all the rest put together was that to the girls he was still the same loving, compassionate person he had been right from the very start, underlining for her, if she had needed that doing . . . that it was *her* and *her* alone that brought out the cold distance in him she was now experiencing.

Lissa went to bed early while Joel was still out. She heard him come in and move about the bedroom, preparing for bed. Lying beneath the bedclothes she trembled with aching tension longing for him to turn to her and take her in his arms, but knew even as she did so that she was longing for the impossible. She closed her eyes, squeezing back weak tears. Sooner or later she would have to tell him of her suspicions that she was carrying his child. What would his reaction be? It was impossible to doubt his love for Louise and Emma, and in other circumstances, had she been Marisa for instance, she had little doubt that the news would have overjoyed him. But she was not Marisa, and the fact that she was to have his child would create another tie between them . . . a tie she was sure he would not want. She bit down hard on her bottom lip. If she *was* pregnant there was nothing she wanted more than to have his child . . . but how could she bring it into the world knowing how Joel felt about her?

The first thing Lissa noticed when she woke up was the pure clarity of the light streaming in through the curtains. As she sat up and glanced curiously towards the window, Joel walked in from the bathroom. His hair clung damply to his scalp, moisture beading his bare chest. He had wrapped a towel round his hips and Lissa felt the beginnings of reactionary sensations erupt inside her. It was a physical effort to drag her gaze away from him. Her heart was thudding heavily, her mouth dry.

'I see it snowed during the night,' Joel commented, flicking back a curtain, his comment explaining the unfamiliar brightness. 'Only a couple of inches by the looks of it, but there's more on the way. That means I'll be out most of the day. We'll need to make arrangements for feeding the stock in case it gets worse.'

Over breakfast, Louise's excitement about the snowfall successfully covered the empty silence between them, Mrs Fuller coming and going with toast and coffee. Lissa noticed the dry crackers on her own plate and the weak cup of tea. Thankfully most mornings Joel had left their bedroom before she actually got up, and so far had not noticed her brief bouts of nausea. She couldn't go on ignoring her symptoms any longer though she admitted, deftly preventing Emma from overturning her cereal bowl. She would have to make an appointment to see the doctor.

Once that mental decision had been made it was easier to ring the local surgery and make an appointment, which she did as soon as Joel had left the house. She couldn't go on for much longer with the present situation, and nor could she tell Joel of her suspicions without making any attempt to have them confirmed.

Mrs Fuller had gone out to do some shopping,

taking both girls with her, and when the receptionist offered her an almost immediate appointment, Lissa took it.

As she stepped outside it started to snow again, small flurries at first, increasing in density so that by the time she had reached the main road it was snowing quite heavily. Fortunately there was very little traffic on the road, but when she skidded slightly on one sharp bend Lissa began to wish someone else was driving. Living in London had blinded her to the dangers of adverse weather conditions, and her stomach muscles tensed protestingly as she switched her windscreen wipers on to fast in order to clear her window. The doctor's surgery was in the nearest town, in the opposite direction from the small village where Mrs Fuller had taken the girls, and the road to it was a narrow, little used one.

It was nearly an hour before Lissa reached the small market town. She found an empty space in the surgery car park, and hurried on jelly-like legs towards the building.

She wasn't kept waiting very long. The partner she saw was new to her, a pleasant, quietly spoken woman in her mid forties, who briskly confirmed her own suspicions. 'We shan't know for definite of course, until we get the results back,' she added, 'but from what you've told me there seems little doubt that you are pregnant.'

She went on to discuss pregnancy in general with Lissa and advised her to ring her in a couple of days when they should have obtained the results of her test.

Although she had been in the surgery less than half an hour it had been long enough for the roof and bonnet of her car to become covered in snow, as were her tyre tracks. Huddling deeper into her jacket Lissa unlocked her door and climbed in, trying not to dread too much the drive back home.

A cold, biting wind had sprung up while she was inside, whirling the heavily falling snow into a blinding storm. Crawling along in a low gear Lissa prayed that she would reach home safely. Several times she skidded but on each occasion she managed to control the car before any damage was done. When at last she was on the familiar half mile or so of road that led to Winterly's gates relief poured over her, relaxing her tense muscles. She was just about to turn into the entrance when a Land-Rover turned the corner beyond the gate, heading towards her from the opposite direction. She braked instinctively, gasping with shock as she felt her car start to slide towards the stone wall that encircled the park, knowing that she was helpless to prevent the collision.

Her seatbelt pulled tightly against her body as her front wheels dropped into the ditch, the bonnet of her car screeching horribly against the stones. Part of her was conscious of doors slamming and footsteps coming towards her, but until her door was wrenched open and Joel bent down and across her, releasing her seat belt mechanism, she hadn't realised he was in the Land-Rover.

'What the hell did you brake for?' he demanded grittily, almost pulling her bodily out of the car. 'We'd seen you coming and we were waiting for you to turn into the drive. Didn't it strike you that the Land-Rover is far easier to control in weather conditions like these?'

'I didn't think ... I just reacted instinctively,' Lissa admitted huskily. Now that the initial shock of the impact had worn off she was beginning to feel distinctly odd ... only too glad of the hardness of Joel's chest behind her, as he half carried and half dragged her away from her car.

'Where the hell have you been anyway?'

Conscious of the fact that Joel's companion—one of the tenant farmers was watching them Lissa shook her head, closing her eyes on a sudden wave of sickness. She must have gone completely limp in Joel's grasp because instantly his arms tightened round her, and she heard him swearing under his breath as he swung her up off the ground and carried her towards the Land-Rover.

'I'll take my wife up to the house,' she heard him saying to his companion. 'You see if you can get her car out of the way. Left there it will only cause a hazard.'

Dimly, like someone in a dream Lissa was conscious of Joel shouldering open the Land-Rover door and depositing her on the hard seat, before taking his place next to her. The engine started, its roar filling her senses like the sound of waves pounding on to surf, and then they were jolting down the drive towards the house, each jolt making her shudder and clench her stomach muscles against an increasing need to be sick.

The moment Joel stopped the Land-Rover she scrambled out, making for the downstairs cloakroom.

'You'd better call the doctor,' she heard Joel speaking behind her, his voice curt; angry almost. 'Lissa's just had an accident in her car. I'll take her upstairs and get her in bed.'

She wanted to protest that she was neither deaf nor dumb and moreover, perfectly capable of putting herself to bed, but the bout of nausea had left her too weak to do more than moan a miserable protest, as Joel picked her up and strode towards the stairs.

In their room he placed her on the bed, and stood frowning over her for a few seconds before asking tersely, 'Are you hurt at all? Did you bang your head . . .'

'I'm fine Joel,' she told him weakly, 'it's just the shock . . .' Instinctively her hand went to her stomach, and lay tensely there, but Joel missed the betraying gesture, his eyes on the scene beyond the window.

'What on earth possessed you to take the car out in the first place? Where the hell had you been?' He broke off as Mrs Fuller tapped on the door and came in with a tray of tea.

'I've rung the doctor and he should be out soon.'

A numbing lethargy was creeping over Lissa. All she wanted to do was to close her eyes and go to sleep, but Joel wouldn't let her. He kept on talking to her, demanding to know where she had been. If only he would go away Lissa thought weakly, refusing to answer.

'Lissa you mustn't go to sleep.' His voice was painfully harsh, ringing dauntingly in her ears. 'You might be suffering from some slight concussion . . . Open your eyes . . .'

Wearily she did as he instructed. He looked quite pale, she noted with detached curiosity. He also looked extremely angry. It gave her a certain amount of quiet satisfaction to realise that she had escaped somewhere where neither of these emotions could touch her. Indeed she felt extraordinarily detached herself . . . quite strangely so. She must close her eyes . . .

'Lissa!' The sound of her name exploding beside her with angry vehemence forced her to open them again. Joel's head jerked up and he stared at the window, getting up to go and look out.

'The doctor's arrived, thank God.'

His fervence hurt her, betraying how anxious he was to escape from her presence.

Her door opened and Mrs Fuller came in. Lissa smiled weakly at the doctor. The older woman raised her eyebrows. 'Well now . . . what's all this?' she demanded briskly.

'I had a slight bump in my car,' Lissa began to explain, but Joel over-ruled her, telling Dr Soames what had happened in terse, bitten out sentences.

'She was very sick almost immediately afterwards. I was concerned that there might be some degree of concussion.

'Umm . . . I don't think so,' Dr Soames pronounced examining Lissa's forehead. 'She doesn't seem to have bumped her head at all. More likely to be the nausea was caused by her pregnancy.' She frowned a little and said to Lissa. 'I suggest you spend the rest of today in bed. In my view it's too early yet for your accident to bring on a miscarriage, but we won't take any chances. Any other bumps or bruises?'

Lissa shook her head, unable to look at Joel. He had gone to stand by the window when Dr Soames came in and he was still standing there with his back towards her, the intense rigidity of his spine making her heart sink. This wasn't how she had planned to tell him that she might be carrying his child.

CHAPTER TEN

'WHY? Why the hell didn't you *tell* me?'

They were alone, Dr Soames having left, and Mrs Fuller having tactfully shepherded both girls downstairs. Joel swung round to stare at her. Her head was aching muzzily, and Lissa reflected wryly that fate seemed determined to work against her. How on earth was she to marshal her arguments against Joel when her brain refused to work properly.

'I wasn't sure myself. That's why I went to see Dr Soames this morning. I knew it was something we'd have to talk about but I wanted . . . I wanted to be sure of my facts before we did . . .'

'Sure of your facts . . .' How brittle and angry Joel's voice sounded. He swung round and she saw his face, confused by the grimness of his voice and the pallor of his skin. No doubt it had come as a shock to him to discover that she was carrying his child especially when . . . she bit her inner lip painfully to stop the weak tears from forming and forced herself to face the truth. How could Joel want her to carry his child when in reality he loved Marisa?

'Well it seems now that there's precious little doubt.'

She didn't blame him for being angry, but it wasn't entirely her fault, she reminded herself, trying not to remember the sensation of his hands on her skin . . . his mouth against hers, his heart thudding out its primitive intoxicating message against her body.

'Do you want to abort it?'

Lissa couldn't hide the flash of shocked pain in her eyes, but managed to whisper croakily, 'Do you?' She ought to have been prepared for this, but somehow she had not. It was, after all, the neatest, tidiest solution, but it was not one she could ever agree to. Even if Joel rejected her she still intended to go ahead with her pregnancy.

'No.' His voice was harsh, his head averted so that she couldn't see his expression.

'Neither do I,' she admitted huskily.

'You realise what you're committing yourself to, do you, Lissa?' he demanded, still without looking at her, 'and I don't just mean motherhood. I want to make it quite clear now that there is no way I would ever allow anyone else to take my place in my child's life. I won't divorce you so that you can go to Greaves,' he told her levelly, facing her for the first time.

At first Lissa was too shocked to respond.

'But . . .'

'Don't bother to deny it Lissa. I saw the two of you together in London—remember?'

She bit her lip. It was tempting to allow Joel to go on believing that she was in love with Simon, for the sake of her pride if nothing else, but if she did . . . She thought about the child she was carrying . . . Joel's child . . . life would be difficult enough for it as it was with a father who merely tolerated instead of loving its mother. It was better to tell the truth.

'That was a chance meeting Joel,' she told him quietly, 'I bumped into him in the street the day I went to buy a new dress for the dinner party. I didn't tell you at the time because . . .' She laced her fingers together and stared down at them as fiercely as though they were something she had never seen before, concentrating on them so that she would not have to look at Joel.

'Because . . .?' he prompted, his voice steel soft.

Suddenly she felt totally exhausted, her hands relaxed, her body slumping into the matress. 'Do you really need to ask,' she said tiredly. 'Please let's not play games now Joel . . .'

He was at her side in a second, his fingers cool against her unexpectedly hot forehead, his eyes, in the brief second she allowed hers to meet them, deeply concerned . . . so concerned that she felt she must be hallucinating.

It was pointless feeling pain because he had not denied his involvement with Marisa, what had she in all honesty expected?

'No games,' he promised quietly, 'but we must talk Lissa. I must admit that this was not entirely the outcome I . . . hoped for when . . .'

'When you made love to me,' Lissa supplied tiredly. 'No . . . I think I understand what motivated you Joel.'

A shadow darkened his eyes, and she thought for a moment that he looked almost haunted . . . a trick of the light of course.

'And understanding that . . .'

She cut him off before he could go on to tell her as he undoubtedly would that his own feelings had never been involved on more than a merely concerned level. 'It makes no difference Joel,' she told him curtly, turning her face away from his so that he couldn't see the anguish in her eyes. 'I *am* carrying your child, and we are both agreed that the pregnancy should not be terminated. You don't want us to divorce . . .'

'Do you?' He shot the question at her with explosive force, her head automatically turning so that she could look at him. She had seldom seen him look as he was doing now—as though he were fighting to control his anger.

'I believe that for the sake of the children—the girls as well as our own child—we should stay together but . . .' She bit her lip wondering if she dare tell him that she did not know how long she would be able to go on as they were now without completely breaking down. Every time he went out without telling her where he was going—every night he came home late she imagined him with Marisa. Jealousy was a bitter corrosive emotion and one she would far rather not have suffered from.

'But?' Joel prompted harshly. His eyes glittered almost blackly beneath thick spiky lashes. He seemed to have aged somehow, and as he walked towards the window Lissa recognised an inner tension in his movements that tore at her heart.

'When we were first married,' Lissa began carefully, picking her words with forethought, too aware of the delicacy of the ground she was now venturing on to speak completely openly, 'we managed to get on reasonably well, before . . .'

'Before I made love to you?' Joel interrupted harshly, his face oddly drawn. 'Is that what you were going to say?'

It wasn't, but it would suffice. She had meant before she realised the truth about Marisa, but didn't want to say so. Her pride would not allow her to reveal to Joel how she felt about him, or how jealous she was of Marisa.

'Well if that is all that's worrying you, don't let it. From now on our relationship will be as sexless as that of brother and sister if that is what you want?'

For a moment Lissa almost hated him. What on earth did he expect her to do? Beg for his lovemaking? When she knew he loved someone else?

She turned her face away from him and said quietly, 'I don't think I need to answer that question do I Joel?'

She heard the door slam as he went out and only when she was quite sure he was gone did she release a shuddering breath of tension.

In the days that followed while it couldn't be said that there was a complete return to the easy familiarity that had developed between them in the early days of their marriage, Lissa was conscious that Joel was making an effort to put their relationship back on a more relaxed footing.

Her pregnancy test had been confirmed as positive and it was Joel who insisted on driving her to the surgery and waiting with her until Dr Soames had seen her.

The doctor was reassuringly matter of fact. 'I don't envisage that you'll have any problems. The sickness should start to wear off after the third month.' She went on to discuss various aspects of pregnancy inviting Lissa to ask her as many questions as she cared to. The birth would take place in the small local hospital which had its own maternity wing. 'You'll see round that later,' Dr

Soames told Lissa as she ushered her towards the door. 'Don't forget, any problems . . . give me a ring.'

'I'd thought about taking you out to lunch—by way of a small celebration,' Joel commented when Lissa gave him the news, 'but somehow I didn't think it would be what you wanted.'

Remembering how acutely nauseous she seemed to be almost every time she ate, Lissa agreed, surprised by the sudden withdrawal of his hand from her arm, and the shuttered withdrawn expression on his face throughout the drive back to Winterly.

It had been decided that the girls were too young as yet to be told of her pregnancy at this early stage—plenty of time for that later, Lissa suggested, wondering if now was a good opportunity to ask Joel about redecorating the nursery, but he forestalled her by saying as he parked the car, 'I've been thinking that now you might want your own bedroom.'

He said it abruptly, and Lissa was conscious of a fierce stab of pain. No one knew better than she the loneliness of a double bed when both parties kept strictly to their own side, but to be banished to another room. She felt helplessly bereft, and said unsteadily, 'Don't you think it might seem rather odd . . .? Mrs Fuller . . .'

Joel shrugged. 'It's your decision Lissa, I was only thinking of you.'

She took a deep breath and without looking at him said quietly, 'Then I would prefer to continue as we are,' and before he could say anything she hurried past him and into the house, glad of the noisy attentions of the girls which put a stop to any further intimate conversation.

March died into April and April into May. Louisa had started playschool two mornings a week and Lissa drove her there. She had got to know a couple of the other mothers by sight and life seemed to have settled down into an uneventful routine. Joel was punctilious about returning home for dinner, and about spending most of the evening with her, but Lissa was finding herself increasingly tired at night, only too happy to go to bed early. What Joel did once she had, she daredn't even think about. If he went to Marisa, then she didn't want to know. She knew she was behaving like a coward, but she couldn't help it. To live with Joel as his wife knowing he didn't really love her was agony it was true, but to live without him . . . that would be sheer hell.

On the mornings she took Louise to playschool, Lissa normally also did whatever shopping was needed and then picked up the little girl in time to take her home for lunch. This particular Tuesday they were running a little late as she had got involved in conversation with another mother.

As she walked into the house Lissa heard the telephone ringing, its sharp sound cut off as Mrs Fuller obviously answered it. As Lissa opened the kitchen door she heard Mrs Fuller saying, 'Mrs . . . Oh I'm afraid she's out at the moment.' She caught sight of Lissa and then corrected herself, 'No . . . she's just walked in.'

'Who is it?' Lissa mouthed as she took the receiver.

'A Mrs Andrews.'

The shock was so great that Lissa almost

dropped the receiver. Since the night of the dinner party she had had no contact at all with Marisa. A cold finger of dread touched her heart. Had Joel told Marisa that she was pregnant? It was something she hadn't been able to bring herself to ask him.

Forcing herself to appear calm, she smiled into the receiver. 'Marisa?'

'Ah, Lissa. Good. Is Joel there?'

Lissa's fear grew. 'No, I'm afraid he's not.'

'Oh dear. I need to speak to him rather urgently. I've left Peter ... It's been on the cards for quite some time of course. I should never have married him ... *never*. But then one does such foolish things when one is young ... Joel has always understood.'

A feeling of sick dismay was spreading through Lissa's body. Marisa had left Peter ... and she was making it clear that she now wanted Joel ... Shivering with reaction and sick misery, Lissa managed to say that she would pass her message on to Joel when he came in. The soft satisfaction purring through Marisa's voice tormented her, even when she had replaced the receiver.

'Lissa are you all right?' Mrs Fuller's voice cut through her pain.

She managed to shake off the terrible feeling of pain consuming her, long enough to smile and fib, 'Yes ... yes ... fine ... Just a little bit tired, I think I'll go upstairs and lie down for a while. If Joel comes in could you ask him to ring Mrs Andrews. She wants to speak to him.'

Sleep was impossible, her thoughts a plunging chaos of pain and misery. She had little doubt in her heart that Joel would want to go to Marisa.

How could he not do? But he was tied to her. She would have to let him go. How could she keep him married to her when she knew he loved and wanted someone else? While Marisa had been married their relationship might have stood some chance, but now . . . How could she face herself when she knew that she was the only thing standing between Joel and happiness?

But she was having his child. Her hand cupped her gently curved stomach protectively and deep shudders of anguish racked through her.

She heard Joel's car drive up and forced herself into the bathroom to wash the tear stains off her skin and make herself look presentable. Sooner or later she would have to face Joel, and it might just as well be sooner.

When she went downstairs the study door was open. Joel was standing behind his desk, just replacing his telephone receiver.

'Did you get the message from Marisa?'

How empty and toneless her voice sounded, completely in contrast with the wild fever of emotions inside her.

'Yes, I've just rung her. I'm going to see her this afternoon.' He was frowning, and in the midst of her own anguish Lissa could still feel pain for him. How much he must be regretting now that he had ever married her . . . ever made love to her.

'Mrs Fuller said you weren't feeling well?'

'Just a little tired.' She smiled, hoping he wouldn't notice how plastic a gesture it was. Her face felt as stiff as a mask, her skin drawn too tightly over her bones.

She spent the afternoon with the girls. Emma was growing up quickly and both of them now called her 'Mummy' quite naturally. How would they react to another upheaval in their lives? How would she feel if Joel took them away from her? Tears stung her eyes, and she blinked them away, but not before Louise's sharp eyes had spotted them. 'You're crying,' she accused, and watching the apprehension dawn in the childishly rounded eyes, Lissa sought to reassure her. 'No, I've just got something in my eye,' she fibbed, distracting her attention, but reaching for one of their colourful nursery books and offering to read to them.

It was Mrs Fuller's evening off, and suspecting that it would be some time before Joel returned—after all he and Marisa would have a good deal to talk about—Lissa ate with the girls.

Once they were in bed she wandered restlessly round the sitting room switching on the television but too tense to really watch it.

It was just gone eight when Joel walked in. He looked tired . . . almost to the point of exhaustion she thought as he sank down into a chair.

When she asked him what he wanted to eat he shook his head. 'I ate with Marisa.' He was curt and withdrawn, and although she longed to reach out to him . . . to help him, Lissa admitted with a surge of bitterness that comfort from her was not what he wanted.

His silent, withdrawn mood lasted for several days and then one night just as Lissa was preparing for bed, he walked into their room and said abruptly, 'Lissa, I have to talk to you.'

This was it! The moment she had been dreading ever since Marisa told her she had left her husband. If she was any sort of woman at all Lissa thought bitterly, she herself would have already faced Joel and had the pride to tell him that she was leaving, but she had just not been able to do it.

She had already showered and was in her nightdress, and at the cold shiver of apprehension that ran through her body Joel frowned, reaching for his own robe which he handed to her, with a curt, 'You're cold, put this on.'

The scent of him clung to the fine silk making her shiver more.

She hadn't missed the way he had recoiled from her when their hands had accidentally made contact.

'Lissa, we can't go on as we are doing at present.' He had his back to her, and she was bitterly conscious of the tension inside him. One half of her, because she loved him, sympathised with the agony he was going through the other half, again because she loved him urged her to cover her ears, to shut out whatever painful truths he was now going to tell her.

'It isn't fair on you and it isn't fair on the girls . . .' His words made her mouth tighten bitterly. Whatever she had thought him she had never considered him the sort of man who would make excuses . . . avoid the truth. What he should be saying was that he could no longer endure living with her and not with Marisa, but she didn't interrupt him.

'I know we said we'd make a fresh start—but then I didn't realise . . .' He turned towards her and the white torment of his face shocked her. Instinctively she stepped towards him intent only on comforting him, immediately falling back as she saw the shutters come down, blocking her out, warning her against going to him.

'Well that doesn't matter . . . what I'm trying to say to you is that for all our sakes, I've decided it would be best if we lived apart. I want you and the girls to stay here. I'll move out . . . and of course I'll continue to see the girls . . . and . . . and our child . . .'

'Just as long as you don't have to see me as well,' Lissa managed huskily, turning away from him so that he wouldn't see her tears.

'For God's sake don't make this harder for me than it already is!' She could feel the anguish within him, see it as his body literally shook with tension. His face was white and drawn, his eyes glittering febrilely.

What could she say? How could she plead with him to stay when she knew that he didn't love her.

'I know this whole situation is my fault,' he said bitterly. 'I'm the one who carries all the blame. I forced you into marriage with me. I was arrogant and stupid enough then to think I could make it work. I was even arrogant enough to believe that I could . . .' He broke off and stared into space for several seconds before demanding huskily, 'Just tell me one thing Lissa, that first time I made love to you . . . I . . .'

'You were acting on purely humane grounds?' Lissa supplied for him emotionlessly. 'You were trying to make me feel like a woman and not a child because you felt you had some sort of responsibility towards me? Yes, Joel I realise all that.'

For a moment there was silence and then he asked jerkily, as though unable to suppress the question, 'And did I Lissa . . . did I make you feel like a woman?'

She could see that he was suffering and all her

love for him welled up inside her. 'Yes,' she admitted softly. 'Yes, Joel you did.'

She moved towards him again and he stepped back awkwardly, the first movement she had ever seen him make that wasn't completely co-ordinated. 'For God's sake don't touch me.' The harsh demand splintered her self-control, wiping her face clean of the mask of calmness she had assumed; pain registering in her eyes, her fingers curling closed as she cringed back from him and stumbled towards the door.

'Lissa. No . . . no . . .!' Joel reached the door before her, his arm barring her flight. 'I'm sorry . . .' He leaned against the door and dropped his head into his hands. 'I didn't mean . . . don't look at me like that. I'm sorry . . . It's all my fault, but I genuinely did think we could make it work. I knew when I married you that you didn't love me, but I felt sure there was some spark of desire . . . something we could build on, and then when I discovered the truth . . . It was arrogant and unforgivable of me to believe that because I was your first lover I could use that to tie you to me. Look . . .' He straightened up and looked at her. 'I can't take any more right now. These last weeks . . . living with you, sleeping next to you at night . . .' A slow shudder tore through his body. 'I just can't do it any more. If I stay there's no way I'm going to be able to stop myself from making love to you . . . no way at all.'

Lissa stared at him unable to believe her ears. *Joel* was saying he wanted *her*? But he loved Marisa, an inner voice warned her. She ignored it, filled with sudden feminine power, moving towards him until she was close enough to touch him, placing her palms against his chest, feeling the uneven drum-beat of his heart.

'Lissa.' He groaned her name, burying his face in her hair, his arms coming round her, imprisoning her against his body. His mouth found her throat and explored the satin soft skin roughly, passion bringing a hectic throb to his pulse. He raised his head reluctantly and looked at her, his eyes glittering fiercely. 'I want you Lissa,' he told her rawly, 'and if you don't stop me now . . . If you don't send me away, there's no way I'm going to be able to stop myself from touching you. For years I've wanted you . . . alternated between desire and dislike for you. Did you know that?'

Lissa shook her head, quivering as his mouth feathered across her cheek and touched the corner of her own.

'We hardly ever saw one another,' she managed to croak, unable to believe what she was hearing.

Joel laughed harshly. 'Because I took great care that we should not. It appalled me that I should be attracted to you, especially knowing what I did about you. Me . . . a man of going on twenty-three had fallen head over heels in love with a promiscuous child of fifteen.'

'What?' Lissa pulled away from him to look at him. 'But Joel.'

'Ridiculous I know, and I soon managed to convince myself that I was imagining it. I pushed you out of my mind . . . told myself I was suffering from some sort of delayed adolescent crush, but when John and Amanda died and I was faced with the prospect of seeing you marry someone else I knew I couldn't let it happen. I wanted you for myself, and so I used the threat of taking the children away from you ...'

She was quivering with a strange sensation of everything being totally unreal. Joel in love with her? She couldn't believe it ... and besides ...

'But Marisa,' she managed to demand. 'What about Marisa?'

He frowned down at her. 'What about her?'

'I thought ... you ... she ... I thought you were lovers,' Lissa told him quietly, 'I also thought tonight you were trying to tell me you wanted to leave me so that you could be with her.'

His stunned incredulity might have been almost funny in other circumstances, but when Lissa thought of the agony she put herself through believing him in love with the other woman she felt closer to tears than laughter.

'Marisa is the wife of a friend of mine and that's all,' he told her firmly. 'Okay, once I went out with her, and I agree she might sometimes have given the impression that there was more between us than there genuinely was, but that's all there is to it.'

'But you went to see her ...'

'To help her sort out somewhere to live and give her some financial advice. I also suggested that she think again about leaving Peter.

'But all those evenings when you went out ...'

'I drove around in the car because it was the only thing I could think of to do to keep my hands off you. Lissa after I'd made love to you it suddenly struck me how selfish I'd been. You said I'd acted humanely. Well maybe you see it that way, I don't. I wanted to free you from the trauma of the past yes, but do you honestly think for one moment that if I hadn't loved you as much as I do that I would have done that by making love to you? Couldn't you tell when I touched you how I felt about you?' His hands cupped her face, his expression so tender, so revealing that her heart seemed to stop beating. 'I had to leave you alone after that night. I had to give you at least a chance to re-assess our relationship without the additional pressure of any sexual demands from me. I had to give you the opportunity to do at least some of the experimenting you never had the opportunity to do as a teenager. When I saw you with Greaves I feared the worst . . . and then when you didn't tell me you'd seen him.'

'It wasn't my meeting with Simon I was trying to hide from you,' Lissa admitted with a rueful smile, 'it was the fact that I'd gone especially to London to buy a new dress, purely because I wanted you to admire me in it. When I thought that Marisa was your mistress—the true love of your life, I couldn't bear to admit the truth to you in case you guessed . . .' She broke off, and Joel prodded softly.

'In case I guessed what?'

'That I love you.'

He studied her face silently for so long that she began to think she had imagined it all . . . that he didn't love her at all . . . that it was all a cruel trick but then he bent his head, his mouth gentle on hers, and then less gentle as he felt her response.

'I couldn't believe it when I found out you were carrying my child,' he told her huskily when he released her. 'I thought you must hate me because of it . . . because it would prevent you leaving me for Simon.'

'And I thought you would hate me because it would prevent you from going to Marisa,' Lissa admitted. 'You were so different from the ogre I'd always imagined you to be,' she told him dreamily. 'So tender and caring that how could I avoid falling in love with you? Then you changed, and reverted to the man I'd always thought you were. I thought it was your way of telling me that you did not want any emotional commitment from me. I thought you'd guessed how I felt about you, and that your coldness towards me was because you didn't want to encourage my feelings.'

'Whereas in reality it was directed at myself. The fact that I'd made love to you, quite deliberately . . . in the hope of making you want me physically and then emotionally, destroyed all the previously conceived notions I held about myself. In any other man I would have ruthlessly condemned what I had done.'

'You mean seducing me with champagne and kisses,' Lissa laughed softly and gave him a coquettish smile. 'Oh I don't know . . .' Happiness bubbled up inside her. 'I rather enjoyed it!'

'Oh did you indeed?'

There was nothing in the soft way he murmured the words to cause her heart to jolt into an accelerated beat, but Lissa wasn't really listening to what he was saying, she was too busy looking into his eyes and reading the very private and explicit message they were holding for her.

Joel glanced at his watch and then smiled teasingly at her. 'It's just gone nine. Too early to go to bed do you suppose?'

'Oh definitely!'

'Umm. Well then I shall just have to insist that we finish our fascinating discussion in the privacy of our own room. What do you say to that?'

'I say that it sounds like an extremely good idea,' Lissa confirmed innocently, teasing amusement gleaming in her eyes.

As he slipped his arm round her and propelled her towards the stairs she paused, watching the quick frown touch his forehead.

'Something wrong?'

'Nothing at all,' she assured him. 'I was just wondering if we had a bottle of champagne anywhere.'

Coming Next Month

887 LOVE ME NOT Lindsay Armstrong
A schoolteacher prepares to lead on an Australian boat designer. That's what he did to her sister, after all! But she doesn't count on his infinite charm—and her sister's deceit!

888 THE WINTER HEART Lillian Cheatham
After taking the blame for her sister's tragic carelessness, an artist escapes to Colorado to work as a secretary—never dreaming that her new boss chose her specifically.

889 A VERY PRIVATE LOVE Melinda Cross
While covering an Egyptian Arabian horse show in Kentucky, a reporter traveling incognito uncovers a reclusive American entrepreneur, also in disguise. He's the man she's been waiting for—to make or break her future.

890 THE OVER-MOUNTAIN MAN Emma Goldrick
A motorist stranded in the Great Smoky Mountains seeks refuge at the home of an inventor who imagines she's in cahoots with his aunt to end his bachelor days. What a notion....

891 THE MAN IN ROOM 12 Claudia Jameson
What with the blizzard and the flu epidemic at her mother's Welsh country inn, the man in room twelve is too much. And for the first time in her life, Dawn loses control of her emotions.

892 DARKNESS INTO LIGHT Carole Mortimer
The security-conscious new owner of the Sutherland estate warns his gardener against falling in love with him. But the only danger she can see is that he might break her heart....

893 FOREVER Lynn Turner
Can a surly ex-army colonel and a bogus nun find love and lasting happiness? Perhaps, with the help of a guardian angel to get them through the jungle alive!

894 A MOMENT IN TIME Yvonne Whittal
The shock of seeing each other again shatters the composure of a divorced couple. For her, at least, love lasted longer than a moment in time, though she isn't so sure of him.

Available in June wherever paperback books are sold, or through Harlequin Reader Service.

In the U.S.
901 Fuhrmann Blvd.
P.O. Box 1397
Buffalo, N.Y. 14240-1397

In Canada
P.O. Box 2800, Postal Station A
5170 Yonge Street
Willowdale, Ontario M2N 6J3